CHECK MATE

Michelle Knight

CHECK MATE

DOUBLE DRAGON

Preface

Comedy Science Fiction is one of my loves; I'm a particular fan of shows like Futurama. You can't beat a good laugh and I've written a few pieces of fan fiction over the years. I'm also a bit of an arms-length fan of artificial intelligence. These last few years have seen many things said by many people but fundamentally, I believe we are a long way from a Terminator/Skynet type of world with our current technology.

As my many years in Infornation Technology have seen me go from programmer, to hardware engineer and then on to support, networking and telecoms, I hope you will believe me when I say that I've seen people instruct machines to do some fairly dumb things throughout my career! Many problems are down to human error, or as we say in I.T., it's a, "Pebcak," fault ... Problem Exists Between Chair And Keyboard. Also sometimes known as an, "I.D.10.T," issue.

I.T. has its own unique sense of humour, like the old joke, *"There are only 10 types of people in the world. Those who know binary and those who don't."* or the deliberate misquote, *"There are lies, damned lies, and benchmarks."* You need a sense of humour to survive a career in computing!

In short, a number of my personal experiences and viewpoints have collided to create this novel, so I hope you enjoy it.

As usual, thanks are due to a number of people, so here I say a massive, "thank you," to Jo-Anne, Ruud Paulissen, Diana Persaud, "Studmuffin" *(yes, that's how he wanted to be credited!)*, Dawn Dean, Michael Reed, Siobhan Thomas and, as usual, all who wished to remain anonymous, for their help in making this book.

Extra special thanks to Phillip Kettless for the pocket ammunition thought and to Sean E Graham for the most unusually flavoured doughnut I've ever heard of! The last special thanks goes to Christian Hlasek for the cover design.

Thanks also extended for the 2024 re-write to Kerri Coombs and Phillip Kettless *(yes, he willingly subjected himself to the story twice!)*

Chapter 1
Fangs of the HYDRA

The audience sat in darkened silence. Roughly thirty people of various governmental ranks were housed in a purpose built viewing area behind a thick shield of curved, hardened glass. The tension among those assembled was high, their pulses raised. Secret complexes in the Nevada Desert brought with them a certain degree of fear, awe and wonderment before a person even set foot in them, no matter how experienced they were at doing deals within their walls. These expectant souls were here for a purpose, to view the results of many years work and the spending of a considerable amount of taxpayers money. Their current inability to see anything beyond the glass itself simply made them all the more nervous about whatever was to happen next.

Three large widescreen monitors, positioned above the display window, came to life and the A.M.A.R.S. logo faded up from the blackness. As the logo grew in brightness, the mutterings of the audience faded.

An announcement system crackled into life and a male voice began its spiel. "Ladies and gentlemen. Welcome to the A.M.A.R.S. desert demonstration facilities. Without further ado, may I introduce the latest in military robotic warfare. The Holistic, Yare, Deployable, Robotic Assailant, or H.Y.D.R.A. for short."

One audience member leaned to a colleague.

"What the heck is a Yare?" he asked.

His colleague waved a sales brochure at him. "It's not a thing; it's a description. Agile. Lively. Prepared. Did you actually read up on this thing, or did you only come for the free buffet?"

"Err..." said the man, slightly embarrassed and still none the wiser.

Lights beyond the glass flicked in to life. The audience found themselves staring into a large, white arena that could comfortably hold a major show jumping event. In the middle stood a large, box-like wheeled robot painted an uninspiring dull grey. It was a little larger than a generous four person golf buggy. It wasn't the most awe inspiring of machines. It had a foreboding presence, but it still looked like an oversized tin can on wheels. When the A.M.A.R.S top brass had first seen the HYDRA they had commented on its disappointing looks. The response they received from the design team was that death doesn't wear lipstick, high heels and a corset.

Each corner of the HYDRA had a wheel unit fitted with bulky, knobbly tyres that looked like they could run over a river of molten lava and shrug it off. Dark, straight lines on the body told them that it was heavily segmented and was probably capable of folding itself into various configurations.

The voice continued, "Lets deal with the yare aspect first. One of the most impressive things about this unit is its speed and response." The monitors showed a rotating diagram of the robot and zoomed in on the wheels. "The wheels are powered by high torque electric motors. Despite its weight, it can move quickly from a standing start and achieve impressive speeds. The wheels have independent suspension and can run on rough terrain. There are metal ribs inside the tyres and also foam reinforcement, so if you try and shoot them out they'll continue to run. When this thing gets rolling, it's difficult to stop."

On cue the robot extended and contracted its wheel units independently of each other as if it was trying to bust a move on the dance floor. Then a sensor array roughly the shape of a persons head, rose out of the main body, giving it a hauntingly human-ish look. It then turned rapidly on the spot in both directions and raced around a series of obstacles in the arena.

Dotted around the floor were sets of steps, concrete bollards, lump and bumps of all manner. The HYDRA took them all in its stride at a blistering pace, as it raced around at a rate which was shocking given its size and implied weight. It did three laps of the obstacles before returning to its place in the centre of the arena, its sensor array still unpacked and looking menacingly at the people in the gallery.

The rotating graphic on the screen changed to display the robots head. There were sensors and cameras behind various protective plates of different shapes and colours. "The system doesn't have one central processing unit, instead it has several each with its own purpose. The separate sensors interpret and distil down their own inputs, leaving the central unit to simply control high level behaviour and make overall decisions. The core gets all its information pre-chewed in a manner of speaking. The head, for example, has motion and recognition units which are combined with a multi-frequency communication array that talks with a mainframe back at the control centre. The robot is powerful, but it can only store and process a certain amount of information. Watch closely, because this is going to be fast." The screens switched to a confusing matrix display of what was happening on each of the robots sensors.

From one side of the arena a man started running. The robot sensed the motion and looked at the man. A blistering array of red lines, squares and icons flashed rapidly on the monitors. In a swift action, the robot gave chase. Two arms snapped out from its body and clamped around the man's wrists. The audience could only see him yell with pain as the robot brought both his arms down, forced them behind his back and into a newly opened hole in its body. A moment later, the robot let him go and he fell forwards to the ground, his wrists secured with what looked like a cable tie. A second man in uniform then entered the arena, picked the first man up from the floor and escorted him out.

"Now, let's look at that again in slow motion."

The monitors wound back and replayed what had just happened. The voice took them through the recap. "You can see it detecting a presence and it turns its sensors to pick up a visual image." Red boxes appeared on the screen to highlight the person's head. "It waits until it can see enough of the face to determine an identity. The blue light you see is transmission to the mainframe for identification and then it receives the instruction that this man is not authorised to be in the area. The HYDRA already has a standing order to apprehend such people and report back."

The rectangles changed position on the video feed. "The unit then locates the man's arms and moves to capture him, just above the wrist line. When it has him gripped, it does an analysis of his skeletal structure." Green lines appeared over the man's image, highlighting the elbows and shoulders, "Then it calculates how to get his wrists into the capture unit, where it ties his wrists together. Note that even after it has done this, the identity light is still red."

There was a pause in the announcement as the slow motion video continued to show the man falling not so gracefully to the floor. Then the uniformed man was seen entering the room "The motion detector triggers again and the same exercise is repeated, but this time the mainframe returns a green light to indicate an authority figure and it stands down. It then lets the arrested man be led off."

The monitor snapped back to the external, diagrammatic view of the robot's head. "Being able to talk back to the mainframe is what makes this unit so flexible. It can operate autonomously if you provide pre-loaded targets, but having access to a larger information library is a real power boon. It can tap into a variety of frequencies and can even use domestic mobile phone circuits if it has to. When deployed in a war zone you'll need to supply a communications pod for the best response."

"Now to demonstrate the offensive and defensive capabilities. Please remain seated." The reason for the glass being curved became obvious as the room started to rotate. The arena slid away, to be replaced with a view of the desert outside. There were a number of other robots in front of them, one deliberately positioned to be looking straight at them.

"The units are equipped with a number of weapons." The monitors changed to display an image of the whole body of the robot in its, "human," stance, like the one which was now staring at them through the window. "It has some short distance rockets for destroying doors and moving vehicles, coupled with a very small number of long range rockets for surface-to-air work, such as in aerial pursuit." As the announcer continued to talk, various pods opened and closed, both on the robot in front of them and also on the model on the screens. "Most of its offensive weaponry is based on traditional ordnance but the rounds are a little more specialist to help it penetrate armour."

"It also has a small number of other tools like gas canisters and a capture net, along with tracking beacons. If a target gets in a car or helicopter for escape, it can fire one at the vehicle and follow it beyond line of sight for a few miles, or make the decision to shoot before the target goes out of range."

"If you remember your NASA vehicles, the Curiosity rover was powered by a plutonium carbide battery. That's what we're using in the HYDRA, with the necessary shielding of course.

Now, however, we are able to turn more of the radioactive heat into usable energy. It's enough to power the whole system, performing constant high speed manoeuvres for a number of weeks. Obviously if you're using it on a stealth assignment then that kind of power enables the system to work autonomously for considerably longer than that."

From one side out of sight of the audience, a grenade was thrown next to the robot. When it exploded there was a flash that most of them recognised as an EMP grenade. "Being electronic in nature, it's important that the system is protected from energy fields. While it won't survive a large nuclear explosion it can absorb most infantry deployable EMP weapons."

The demonstration went on for another two hours. The audience watched as the HYDRAs chased smaller robots around, shooting some, entangling others in nets or otherwise just blowing them to bits. Despite the protective glass the audience could still feel the heat of some of the explosions. They were also introduced to a cute little mini-robot that the HYDRA could send up narrower flights of domestic stairs to do odd bits of assassination and reconnaissance work.

At the end of the show the audience were turned around to face the arena again, still proudly displaying the first robot, and the announcer brought the event to a close. "One last thing, ladies and gentlemen; the system is capable of self destruction if necessary, but we'd rather not demonstrate that feature to you for obvious reasons." A chuckle came from the audience, most of whom were now wondering where the toilets were. "Thank you for taking your time today to review the A.M.A.R.S. H.Y.D.R.A. unit. We look forward to taking your orders in the near future."

The lights came up and the audience were led away as the robots trundled back to the maintenance bay.

It was a large, bright white hanger about a mile away from the demonstration field. On the floor were ten white lined areas. These were parking spaces for the robots and each space had plenty of room so that routine maintenance could be done without having to move them. One wall had a glass panel, behind which was a control room housing various terminals and computers. Another had a large, corrugated vertical door and it was through this that all ten robots now trundled and rolled themselves into their lined areas. Once in position they extended their wheel bases for examination, unwrapped themselves into, "human," configuration so that their torsos were exposed, extended all their limbs and opened up the maintenance doors to the central control units. With that, they waited for instruction.

Andy was from Philadelphia on the east coast. His paternal grandparents had moved to America from Europe but by the time he was born, there was no real family connection to speak off across the pond any more. He'd taken industrial design in PhilaU and then bummed around a little before taking a graduate course in robotics through Pennsylvania State University. He had made enough waves with his academic results to bring him to the attention of a scout who worked for American Materials And Robotic Systems. The scout then persuaded him to join AMARS and he had become a part of the HYDRA project.

If Andy had realised that he would effectively be moving to Nevada in order to babysit a bunch of robots, then he would have politely declined the offer; advanced as they were. He was less than enthused about his work and generally had a somewhat defeated aura.

He emerged from the control room, an underwhelmed twenty-something, married to the job with no sex life and loads of overtime to his name. The only unremarkable thing about his gait was that his left hand was twitching slightly, which it did when he was nervous. Whenever the robots came back still carrying live ammo he got the jitters. Although anyone would be understandably nervous when working with live ordnance, Andy had reason to be more scared than most.

It was early days with the Hydra units. Everything was perfectly fine until one fateful day when he was working on the chest panel of one of the machines. To help him get a better grip, he had one arm wrapped around the side of the robot. When his screwdriver slipped and caused an electrical short, one of the rocket bays shot out of the side. Andy's arm was taken with it and it jammed his clothing in the mechanism so he couldn't free himself. He had suddenly found himself nose to nose with a bank of live rockets; his bright white underpants becoming a mushy mixture of brown and yellow as abject terror gripped his body. Even though the hanger was very large and the bay doors were closed, his screams were clearly audible outside the building.

As there was a risk of setting off a rocket, it took three people to free him and by that time he had become a nervous wreck. Eventually they had managed to get the jellied, shivering Andy on to a stretcher and off to hospital. Despite the successful extraction, however, it was more than a month before he returned to work and even then he restricted himself to lab duty. It would be another six weeks before he had the courage to return to the HYDRA hanger and be in the presence of the robots again. Although the team tried their best to limit the times when the Hydras were in the hanger while armed, occasions like this were unavoidable.

Gary followed Andy from the control room. It was just the two of them; the lone tidy-up crew. After successful demonstration runs like these it was accepted that the rest of the team would go off to celebrate a hard-earned victory, leaving Gary and Andy to clean up and join the rest later.

In his mid thirties, Gary was from Sacramento just a little further up the west coast. He had taken computer science and followed it up with a masters in electrical engineering. This made him another ideal candidate for the Hydra babysitting team. Despite his age he still hadn't grown out of his early college habits. His main means of relaxation was stuffing copious amounts of pizza and drink down his neck, while watching action and horror films; or playing on his games console and swearing at the screen. He wore brightly coloured shirts and called everyone, "dude," including the women, which didn't go down well among the AMARS staff. That probably explained why he, too, was still single.

His mix of everyday surf culture slang and film curses confused the hell out of everyone who knew him. If you stuck a surf board under his arm then he looked like a classic, west coast American surfer. However, to the best of everyone's knowledge he had never so much as waxed a board in his life, let alone ridden one. He hadn't even driven a woodie. No one could figure him out. Regardless of where he obtained his mannerisms, his attitude and language were, perhaps, why he had been stuck at this level in AMARS for so many years. Not that he cared, to be honest. He had enough money for beer and pizza along with the free time to devour it, so he was cool. That was all he asked for in life.

Andy, however, still had dreams of rising to greater things. His plan of climbing the technical ladder was being scuppered by his tendency to become a stuttering jelly whenever the robots were armed. Unfortunately, this usually coincided with the occasions when their superiors paid a visit. Thus he never got the chance to impress anyone in power and he was starting to believe that he'd be stuck working with Gary in the hanger for the rest of his life. Needless to say this was a prospect which didn't fill him with much glee and further contributed to his already dour demeanour.

Sensing that Andy seemed to be a little more depressed than normal, Gary tried to give him a little encouragement. "Come on, brah. The sooner we're done, the sooner we can get out of here."

"How many times have I got to tell you to not call me brah. I am neither a surfer or Hawaiian."

This hard nosed response bounced off laid-back Gary who had heard it all before. "Come on, dude. It's you and me. We're a team! High five!" Gary placed his hand in the air but as usual, Andy left him hanging and simply grabbed one of the mobile monitoring units. He deliberately wheeled it quite a few feet away from Gary and started tapping at the keyboard.

"Look, can we just get on with this please."

"Sure." Gary smiled, ignoring Andy's negative attitude. He knew his partner in crime hated it when there were explosives around so he didn't mind being blown off. He started going from robot to robot, taking cables that were hanging from the ceiling and plugging them in to the exposed chest cavities.

Andy continued hammering at the console, running diagnostics programs, while Gary moved to a telephone and called the armoury. As the ring-out tone sounded in Gary's ear, he sighed and looked over the machines. Sand everywhere. It would take them ages to clean them down. And the floor. Couldn't do anything about that until the tin cans had been disarmed though.

The phone continued to ring out and Gary looked at his watch. "Oh no. I think we've missed the wave. The armoury's closed."

Andy sighed. "Well that's just great. We're going to have to wait until..." some beeping interrupted him. "Unit six is reporting a problem." Gary put down the phone and joined Andy at the monitoring unit. "Ah. That's it. The memory stick in the control unit's got a fault. Just an unreliable cell in an unused area, nothing serious. We'll have to change it though."

"Flash failure? Wasn't that the bot used for the EMP demo, dude?"

"Yes, I think it was. I'll send an e-mail to the design team. They need to take another look at the EMP protection."

"Sounds cool. We don't have any spare sticks down here though."

"OK, take it out, mark it up and we'll replace it with a fresh stick back at the lab."

Andy finished up at the terminal and filled in some paperwork while Gary went around to each robot in turn, hitting the power buttons on the central units and removing the memory sticks. When it came to number six, he took a red pen out of his pocket and filled in the letter A in the AMARS logo on the stick as a way of noting which one had to be replaced.

With the robots powered down and memory sticks in hand, he approached Andy at the console. "Look dude, you're a nervous wreck. I'll take care of the lab stuff and you go join the team. Yeah?"

Andy sighed. For all his rough edges, Gary was a good soul. "You know, that would be really, um, cool." He tapped the power button on the terminal, handed the completed paperwork to Gary and the pair of them walked in to the glass fronted control room. "Oh, those manuals have to go back as well. You sure you're OK with taking all this?"

"Yeah, no problem. You go chill and I'll be

there in a bit."

"Well, there's no chance of you missing the fun. I heard that the event they've laid on is going to last most of the night."

"Yeah, I heard them talking about the party. It's gonna be sick, dude!" Gary used his free hand to lightly punch Andy on the shoulder. For his part Andy responded by picking up the manuals and handing them to Gary, in the hope that he wouldn't be able to punch or high five him again with his hands full. With everything done and gathered, they left the control room and entered the maze of white corridors that made up the AMARS desert complex with Gary shouting, "Free pizza!" and Andy shaking his head in despair at his colleague.

Chapter 2
Not according to plan

The programming labs were segregated according to security clearance. Gina Hicks and Tom Williams were sat in one of the lowest status labs in the facility. Both were early twenty-somethings who wanted to be big names in mathematical research and were currently part of a small team working on improving the code to play chess.

Making computers more efficient at chess wasn't, in itself, one of AMARS high level goals. While people recruited by the scouts generally started on useful work, people who came in by the usual application process had to be tested before they were let lose on anything that had the potential to go bang. Working on chess programs was a way for new staff to cut their teeth in advanced analytical thinking. AMARS could also see how well they worked in a team and whether they fitted in with the company way of doing things.

It was a relatively sparse lab. A number of terminals were dotted around, along with chess sets in various states of play. There was also a, "team table," in the centre. A poster of IBM's Deep Blue computer was stuck on one wall, along with various chess heroes like Karpov, Kasparov and Fischer. Each of the four teams that operated in the lab had its own white board and they were all filled with assorted scribblings. Pride of place, however, was given to a small wall board with the four team names on it. Beside each name was a performance score made up from the time that their latest algorithms had taken to complete a winning game, weighted with the size of the programs they had created. Faster and smaller resulted in a better score. There was a small cash prize at the end of each month along with the chance for the strongest team to be elevated to other duties in the company.

A tall book-case stood off to one side that held classical works from the likes of Vincent, da Cutri and Stamma. They rubbed spines with modern opinion on mathematics and programming technique. Some of these books were also in use, dotted around the lab and held open by coffee mugs, pencils, or whatever was to hand at the moment that something was needed to hold a place.

Gina and Tom were getting excited about a new twist that they had worked into their latest algorithm. It had cost them a few bytes of extra code, but they thought it might gain them precious processing time. They were the only people in the lab; working late because they were close to a breakthrough and didn't want to lose their thread.

Gina was the team leader and desperately wanted to move on from working on chess. "I really want to snatch the winning place with this one." she said, practically itching with excitement.

"Cool down." said Tom, parking his pencil behind his ear so he could type faster. "No one's going to die over this."

"Come on, you know that this could be our ticket out of here."

"Only if we're right. We could always be wrong

you know."

"No. I've got a feeling in my bones about this. What we've done here is going to take us in to the lead, I'm sure of it." She was practically bouncing on the chair with nervous energy.

"There. It's compiled. Pass me a memory stick."

Gina fumbled in a small drawer of sticks. They were standard AMARS issue complete with security tags. They were designed to set off alarms if people tried to take them off campus. Because of this, however, they all looked exactly alike except for a marker which stated the capacity. "I want to make sure I don't get this mixed up like last time. That screw up cost us a place on the board."

Tom sighed. "Put a dot on it or something."

"Good idea." She picked up a red marker and filled in the hole in the first letter "A" on the logo before handing it to Tom. He inserted it in to the workstation and transferred the compiled code. Then he read it back to verify it had written correctly. Even though it only took a matter of moments, Gina was wiggling her feet in anticipation. She looked at her watch. They didn't have much time left before the mainframe operative would leave for the evening and if they missed that window then they'd have to wait until morning. Like Tom had said, no one was going to die over this but Gina wanted to go home with a success under her belt.

Gary, in the mean time, had entered the programming lab corridor with his arms full of manuals and paperwork. He was bound for the high security area but as he passed the chess lab, the door opened and a highly strung Gina rushed out, colliding with him. They both uttered surprised gasps and dropped everything they were carrying.

"Whoa dude. Wipe out. Not cool."

"I'm sorry." stammered Gina, as they both started shuffling around on the floor to collect their stuff. "I'm in a hurry."

"No kidding."

Gina only had her folder and memory stick to recover. She quickly found the stick and after apologising to Gary again, she left him to pick up his own things while she made a dash for the mainframe room.

Whenever the teams had finished their programs and wanted to test them, a standard, supervised routine would be run to determine how well they performed. That way no one could cheat the system. Gina ran up to the door but it didn't open. She peered through the glass but the operator's chair was empty. "Damn!" she had missed them and would have to wait until tomorrow after all.

Back in the corridor, Gary picked up all his bits and pieces and continued on through the various security barriers. He was relieved to finally make it to the Hydra lab. He deposited the now mixed pile of papers and manuals on the table and searched among the sticks for the one with the red dot. With the faulty memory stick in hand he went over to the drawer where they kept the unused ones. He needed a sixty four gig module but the largest he could find was thirty two. "Not cool." he said to the empty room. They'd just have to re-use the faulty stick tomorrow and place an order for more stock.

Using his security card and thumb print he opened a drawer that was reserved for the programmed keys and put them all away safely. Then he tidied up the paperwork, placed it in a secure cabinet and left to join the party. Free pizza. Now there was something to celebrate!

The event itself took place in a purpose built hanger on the AMARS complex. It had been fitted with a top quality DJ area, disco lights, flashing dance floor and an impressively stocked bar. At one end there was even a shallow swimming pool and fake palm trees for Hawaiian nights.

Adjacent to this were sound-proofed sleeping quarters that, despite only being used once or twice a year, had been built with considerable thought and effort. As far as the company was concerned the investment was worth it for two simple reasons.

Firstly it made sense that when the chief scientists and other important people were going to get mind blowingly drunk, that they did it in a safe environment where there was no chance of them divulging any secrets to the competition.

Secondly it was a simple fact that you didn't find many nightclubs in the Nevada Desert.

There was also rumour that it saved AMARS considerable embarrassment. While their staff were among the most intelligent, well paid, high academic achievers in the country, it was a sad fact that most of them couldn't dance to save their diplomas.

Each room had its own small en-suite and there

was a mini bar stocked with fresh milk and water along with packets of various tablets, sachets and capsules. If someone became violently ill they could endure their self imposed trauma without upsetting anybody else and had all the tools they need to recover from the hangovers, stomach pains and other ailments that human beings suffered after getting completely smashed out of their skulls on alcohol.

By the time that Gary walked in, the party had been in full swing for some time. He looked around for Andy but he was lost in the sea of people. A long table off to one side was being continually filled and then emptied of food. Pizza, cheese sticks, burgers and lots of party snacks that were so brightly coloured that they probably came with health warnings. If it wasn't immediately recognisable or at least labelled, then it was best avoided.

Being a scientific community they had designed their own plates specially for these events. He picked one up, hit it over his knee and started to load it with pizza. The plate was a form of plastic that was filled with luminescent chemicals, just like night sticks. Not only was it firm enough to withstand the weight of fat laden foodstuffs, but the action of giving it a healthy whack caused the liquids inside the plate to mix. This had the dual purpose of giving off heat, so your food stayed warmer for longer, and as long as you remained sober enough to remember what colour your plate was, it would call out to you from across the darkest of dance floors. Tonight, his was bright lime green. Not a good colour choice to go with egregious over consumption.

Despite the number of people packing out the hall, Gary enjoyed ease of movement. His reputation was such that even when people were very much the worse for wear, they could always recall a subconscious need to avoid him. As a result people would make a path for him wherever he wanted to go. Usually, it was a straight line between the food table and the bar.

Although things went well and started to run into the small hours, this particular party was destined to finished earlier than some. A chief scientist from one of the chemical labs was on the illuminated dance floor during a particularly popular track. For a reason known only to him and some now-dead brain cells, he decided that he would attempt an impressive dance move that he'd seen John Travolta do in a film. When an appropriate up-beat came along, he put one hand on his waist, sent his hips violently out in one direction and flung his other hand out to the side. Because his alcohol-addled brain had failed to account for the proximity of other dancers, he promptly smacked one of the AI programmers in the jaw with his clenched fist.

It wasn't so much the force of the punch but more the surprise factor that led the drunken programmer to stop doing, 'the macarena,' and begin a very short burst of, 'sack of potatoes,' as he hit the deck and found himself laying there, looking up at the glitter ball thinking, 'Oooh! Pretty!'

Officially the security guards were supposed to be there to make sure that no one got hurt, but most of them volunteered for party duty so they could have a laugh at the pathetic dancing. Tonight, however, they actually had to do some work. The music was stopped, the house lights brought up and staff members in various states of inebriation had to be herded like cattle to the sleeping quarters.

Chapter 3
Kings pawn to E4

Gina was in early the following day. Bright eyed and bushy tailed, memory stick in hand, she was pacing outside the door to the mainframe room, waiting for Bill to turn up.

"You're in early." said Bill from nowhere, causing her to jump.

"Jeepers. You scared the hell out of me." she responded, putting one hand on her racing heart.

"Well, you were staring so intently at your feet that I didn't rightly know any other way of getting your attention." He looked her up and down. She appeared to have been main-lining caffeine. Bits of her were twitching and her eyes were wider than saucers. "You OK?"

"Yes, yes, just got to get this thing tested, that's all." she eagerly held up the memory stick almost as if she was expecting Bill to read its contents by sight alone.

"Oh. Another test." He was a seasoned veteran of the AMARS mainframe facility and the sight of the stick relaxed him a little. It explained exactly why Gina was behaving like a startled meerkat on drugs. She had another program on which her career hopes were pinned. "You really think this one's your ticket out of the chess labs, yes?"

"I'm certain of it!" she replied with confidence and gusto.

"Ok, well, lets get in and settled then." Bill swiped his ID on the card reader and as the door vanished sideways with a gentle sigh, he gestured with his arm. "After you." At least if Gina went in before him, she wouldn't see him roll his eyes in despair.

They walked into the operator's area which was a comfortable room with various consoles and three chairs. Bill sat in his regular place and Gina settled into one beside him.

"Right. Bear with me while I log on and get everything running."

Gina kicked her heels while Bill got comfortable and made himself at home. He knew that she was under pressure, but he also knew that it was self-imposed and he wasn't going to get his whole day off to a rushed start simply for her to have her results thirty seconds quicker.

Eventually, he had everything organised and reached out his open hand to Gina. "Stick please." He didn't have to ask twice; indeed he barely got to the end of the first word before the memory stick was in his palm.

Bill inserted it into the mainframe terminal and transferred the program to main memory. "OK, I'm putting this in a sandbox so we can monitor how well the algorithm performs." He tapped on the keyboard like the experienced pro that he was. Gina knew what he was doing but he liked to narrate the process as a mental check that everything was being done correctly. "I'm firing up the move database now." Whenever a program made a move, the database could create a counter move immediately so that the program under test could be stressed as much as possible.

"OK, launching the program now." Gina took a deep breath and Bill hit the run key.

He looked at the terminal in surprise. "It's sucked in the whole damn database!"

"What?" Gina strained to see the output on the screen. "What's it doing with it?"

"Nothing. It's just sitting there waiting for more input."

Gina moved in to Bills personal space so she could see the screen better. "It's not supposed to wait for an instruction. It's supposed to be making a move."

Bill twisted his head and went nose to nose with her, "Well, it obviously ain't doing what you think it should be doing, that much is a cert. Can you back off a bit please?"

Gina sighed and sank back in to the chair. They must have missed something critical but she couldn't see how. "Sorry to have wasted your time on this. I'll take it back to the lab and see what happened."

Bill wiped the running sandboxes, unmounted the stick and returned it to Gina who moped all the way back to the lab, trying to figure out what went wrong. As she walked through the door, Tom was already there. Some people from other teams were milling around the desks at the edge.

"How'd it do?" he enquired.

"It didn't even run."

"What?"

Gina walked dejectedly to the table, shoulders sagging as she told Tom what had happened. "It sucked in the whole move database and just sat there giving no output."

"Well that's not right."

"I know." she said, slumping down in one of the other chairs. "Here. I'm just too down to look. Can you see why it failed?"

Tom took the memory stick from Gina and gave it a look over. "This isn't one of our sticks."

"What do you mean?" She took the stick back off him. "Of course it is. It's got my red dot on it. Look." she pointed at the letter A filled in with red ink.

"No it isn't. That's a sixty four gigabyte stick. Ours are only eight."

They looked at each other, while their minds whirred around the problem. If that wasn't their stick, then what was on it? Also, where the hell was theirs? Gina's memory went straight to the accidental collision with Gary. "Oh hell."

In the Hydra hanger Gary and Andy were doing a full systems check. The armoury said they'd be along in the afternoon to disarm their robots. All that time couldn't be wasted so work had to continue.

Gary re-loaded the memory sticks in to the robots, making a special point to put the failed stick back in to unit six. "How many do you think we need to order?" asked Andy from his usual place at the mobile console.

"Oh, I don't know. Another ten maybe?" Gary shrugged his shoulders. "Do what you think best." He glanced over his shoulder and saw Andy rubbing his forehead in pain. "You OK there dude?"

"I'm fine. Just a little hung over from last

night."

"Yeah," Gary smiled, "That was a wicked party!"

Andy looked at his colleague with puzzlement. "I just don't know how you manage to put away so much alcohol and pizza, and still function like it was nothing."

"Oh, practice; practice." Gary solemnly nodded his head in recognition of the pride he had in himself. "It takes serious effort, you know." The ability to punish the human body with copious slices of calorie rich, artery clogging, baked dough and cheese, wash it down with ridiculous quantities of alcohol, yet still be up and working at the early hours of the same morning in which you finished the self-abuse session, required considerable dedication. It had taken him many years to achieve this feat and that was in spite of several campus medics that had voiced serious objection to his behaviour.

He wasn't going to stop though. Gary was still building up loyalty points from the pizza outlets in town. He hadn't used any of them yet; he wanted to go down in the Guinness Book of World Records for something, but he wasn't entirely sure what. The alcohol had made that bit of his memory a little fuzzy. The only thing he could remember was the desire to stockpile the points.

After completing the order for fresh memory sticks Andy turned his attention to the list of checks they had to do on the robots. Using the faulty memory stick concerned him, but he wanted the ordnance the heck out of the robots. The other members of the team were still sleeping off the effects of the party but he was confident that they'd start turning up soon enough. Or maybe not. No one liked cleaning up after a show.

The robots were still cabled so Andy could wake them from where he was. He called to Gary to get clear and then he turned them on. One by one there was a mild whooshing noise from each robot as they fired up and went through their initialisation cycles. They moved their various joints and extended and retracted the important pieces of their mechanisms.

He hated this. All ten of them going through their start up routines in the otherwise empty warehouse made a heck of a noise. His cowered down behind the small column that contained the mobile terminal and held his hands over his ears, partially because of the din but also because he didn't particularly want to see the part of the display when the rocket racks came out. The deployment and retraction of the sniper rifle and machine guns were also a little scary. Once more he wished he was back on the east coast doing a nice, boring job where the most risk you took was jay walking.

Gary was the opposite. He just stood there, looking at the robots with a grin on his face and a puffed out chest. Oh yes, he liked his toys. This was definitely most cool as he liked to say.

The whole process took about half an hour for basic testing. The tracking systems had to be tested as well, but they needed to move the robots to a special area for that. It was a purpose-built range which had various targets that swung back and forth so the HYDRAs could be seen to follow them, but they dare not do that while the robots were armed with live weapons. There was nothing else for it but to power them back down after the initial tests and wait for the armoury team to show up.

They used to do some of this testing in the hangar until one fateful day when an unfortunate soul forgot the golden rule of checking to see if a robot was still armed before doing a targetting test. James Gregory Thompson was the man's name and there was a brass plaque in his memory, on the entrance to the newly built target range; because there wasn't much left of the old hanger by the time the dust had settled.

As well as reminding people of James' life it also served to remind others of his rather unfortunate and messy demise. From that point on people were a little more thorough in checking the robots before they began any testing.

All games of chess start with the first move. The moment that the white player decides which piece will begin the battle. The opening gambit for this game happened when Andy told Gary, "OK, best turn them off and pull the sticks." Unit six heard this instruction. Gary moved up the line of robots, hitting their soft power switches and disconnecting the cables. Unit six determined that you didn't just stop a game of chess once it was started. Someone had to win and someone had to lose. It decided that its next move was to ignore the power down signal. The game had begun.

When Gary reached it and pressed the button, it stayed on. Gary couldn't quite work this out, so he depressed and held the power button in the hope that this would make a difference. He counted to five but still the unit remained functional. Puzzled, he turned and called to Andy. "This one isn't listening to the power down signal. Any ideas?"

"OK, I'll do it from here." Andy tapped on the terminal but still the unit remained running. "You continue with the others and I'll run some diagnostics."

Gary finished the last four and by the time he had pulled their sticks he looked back to see that unit six was still running. "Still not playing, dude?"

"No. I'm telling it to shut down and it's acknowledging the command, but it's just not actually doing it."

"That's not right." Gary walked up to number six, looked it straight in the chest and scratched his head. "What if I just pull the stick?"

Andy thought about his suggestion. "I honestly don't know what that would do. Probably not a lot as the program is already in main memory."

Gary gave his idea a bit more thought but being out of options, he decided to reach out and remove the memory sick anyway. As his hand got close to the controls, unit six determined that he wasn't playing fair and tried to shut its body panel. It couldn't manage it, however, as the cable was still connected. Gary pulled his arm back sharply and his jaw dropped. "Dude! This thing just tried to shut the panel on me! What gives?"

"Uh, I don't know. It could be a protection thing. Back off from it." Gary did so, and the robot stopped trying to close the panel. However, unit six decided to put a call in to the mainframe for additional information.

"I don't like the way this thing's behaving. Where's the team?"

"Probably still sleeping off the free booze. Not everyone's as skilled as you in self abuse."

"I'm going to try the power button again." Gary approached the robot once more but this time he got an even bigger shock as the unit reached out an arm, unplugged its cable and then shut the panel. "What the hell!"

They both stared, open mouthed at what the robot had done. Andy couldn't comprehend what he was seeing. "I've heard of protection protocols but this is going a bit far."

"We need to get that panel open. This is starting to be seriously not cool."

Andy opened a drawer in the mobile terminal unit and pulled out a screwdriver and a pair of snips. He walked over to the robot as casually as an arachnophobe might approach an obviously pissed off tarantula. As he reached out a very shaky hand to open the body panel, number six reversed away from him.

The two men jumped back in wide-eyed shock. "Dude! Seriously not cool!" Gary exclaimed.

Andy's whole body started to shake in fear as his mind raced to make sense of what was happening. Gary just stood there waiting for someone else to offer any form of insight as he was completely stumped. After a minute or two, his heart still racing, Andy managed to deliver his conclusion on what they were facing. "I think it's waiting for us to make a move."

Gary just looked at him. "Tell me you're kidding. We're stood in front of a heavily armed robot you moron. There IS only one possible move. RUN!"

Andy dropped the tools and the pair of them sprinted through the door to the control room, finding some shelter behind a bank of terminals. Any sane person would have realised that the terminals would offer about as much protection from a heavily armed robot, as a wet piece of tissue paper would stop a speeding bullet; but right now neither of them were capable of thinking straight.

Gary sniffed then looked at Andy. "Oh dude."

"Sorry." was all that Andy could offer by way of apology for the trickle of yellow liquid that was running down his right leg and starting to form a small puddle beneath him.

In spite of the stench of Andy's urine, the prospect of facing off against a heavily armed, misbehaving robot compelled them to stay right where they were; peering out between the terminals. They watched number six through the glass. It just stood there, doing nothing, but they were convinced it was staring right back at them making plans on how it was going to kill them.

"It doesn't make sense." said Andy, once he had regained enough confidence to be reasonably certain that the robot wasn't about to begin an all-out assault on their hiding place.

"It had to be the memory stick dude." Gary volunteered.

"No. The fault was in an unused area of the

stick. There was no part of the actual program stored there." Andy started tapping at one of the terminals, not daring to rise from his crouched position. He called up the diagnostics that he had just done on the robots. "In fact, the fault is gone. This doesn't make sense."

Gary, also unwilling to stick his head any higher than the top of the nearest monitor, looked over Andy's shoulder. He pointed at the screen. "Oh no. Look at the stats!"

"What about them."

"That stick's the wrong size. It's not the right stick."

"It's got to be. It had the same red dot you put on it yesterday, right?"

"Yeah, but..." Gary trailed off.

While Gary was stuck in disbelief, Andy called up the detailed records. Indeed, it wasn't the right stick. The checksums were wrong, the file sizes were wrong, the whole damn thing was wrong. "You're right." he announced. "It's wrong." He waited a few moments and then turned to Gary for any explanation that might be forthcoming.

Gary slapped his forehead. "Oh dude! I crashed in to one of the chess lab people last night. The sticks must have got mixed up."

"Another stick with the same red dot? What are the odds of that?"

"I don't know, but I think that robot is running some form of chess program." Gary picked up a nearby phone and called reception. "Yeah, this is the Hydra bay. Can you put me through to the chess lab please?" he waited a moment. "Yeah, I know they're in the directory but I kinda don't have easy access to one right now." More listening. "Yeah, I … well this is kind of an emergency." He listened to the operator's next statement and put his hand to his forehead. "I know, I know. You've got a point. There aren't many emergencies that require a chess expert but just trust me on this one. Please?" It was probably the desperation in his voice that made the operator believe him, because the next thing that Gary heard was a ringing tone.

"Chess lab."

"Yeah, um, this is the Hydra team. Has one of you guys lost a memory stick?"

At that moment, the door opened and a slightly dulled Professor Hicks entered the room, slopey shouldered and looking the worse for wear from the previous evening. An experienced man of science he took pride in his crisply ironed white lab coat and horn rimmed glasses and, hang over be damned, he still did his best to project a professional aura. What happened next, however, was far from professional and it was probably for the best that last nights party had muted his faculties. Andy immediately shouted, "Get down!" and launched himself at the Professor. The pair of them hit the floor and ended up in a heap behind another bank of terminals.

"Good god man!" spluttered the Professor as he straightened his glasses and attempted to pat down his lab coat. His attention was grabbed, mid complaint, by the sight of Gary kneeling on the floor in front of a terminal, talking on the phone with a panicked look on his face. He turned back to

Andy. "What the hell do you think you're doing?" Then he noticed that Andy was a shivering wreck. "Why are you shaking like that?" That was when the odour hit him and his nose scrunched. "And why does the room smell of urine? Has everyone gone stark raving mad?"

It took five minutes for Gary to bring the Professor up to speed while Andy used foam cleaner to mute the urine puddle, then stuffed his wet trousers in a trash bag and tied it up in the hope of containing some of the smell. Andy was now stood there in just his shirt and underpants, bent over and struggling to put his shoes back on. His fingers were shaking so badly with fear that he felt they could drop off his hands at any moment.

"OK," announced the Professor. "If what you say is correct, then the robot should be perfectly harmless as long as we don't provoke it." He got out of his chair and Gary followed him in to the hanger. They stood a respectful way back from the Hydra. Hicks crossed his arms, then winced, uncrossed them again and used a hand to rub his coccyx which was still hurting after the unexpected take down. "That was a bit of a rough landing, you know." he commented to no one in particular. Having calmed the ache in his lower spine for a while, he re-crossed his arms and turned his attention back to the robot. "Well, I don't know what we're going to do about this. The robots have a very strong reactive intelligence but no actual desire, so we need to be able to think of a way to capitalise on that."

Andy meekly entered the hanger, shamed by his loss of self control. "I'm sorry, Prof. I'm not normally like this." he offered, unable to take his eyes off the robot.

Hicks turned to look at him. "No worry. I appreciate that having this much weaponry around is bound to bring out the worst in some people. Now, kindly man the terminal and get ready to run any ideas we come up with please." When he observed Andy start to comply, Hicks turned back to the robot.

Gary offered the only particular thought that crossed his mind. "What if we just leave it there?"

Andy looked at them both, realised that Gary was serious and then ran the figures. "Um, if it didn't move at all then the power drain of the surveillance systems and minimal processing power would be minute."

"What are we looking at?" queried Hicks.

"Plutonium carbide batteries, minimum drain, approximately a hundred and seventy years."

Gary choked, "A hundred and ...?! Man, we're going to have to work in here with an armed robot for the rest of our careers? How we gonna do that? Wall it in?"

There was a minuscule sound of a motor whirring on number six's monitoring assembly. Andy stated the obvious, "I think it heard you."

Gary stated something even more obvious, "Fuck."

"Now, you two, it seems we're going to have to be very cautious regarding what we say and do around the Hydra. The sensors are interpreting everything and are passing it to the core, after translation."

Andy understood, but Gary didn't. "Not following Prof."

"Come on Gary. You've been babysitting these things since inception. The sensors sit between the core and real world. The core knows nothing more about you other than you're an object. It doesn't know any difference between you or a chess piece. The sensors do a lot of the interpretation work so the core can run as quickly as possible. Image processing, audio, language; all handled by the supplemental modules. All the core does is make action decisions."

A light of realisation came into Gary's eyes as the penny dropped. "So the supporting systems are interpreting the real world for the chess program. If it wasn't for them, it wouldn't be able to make sense of reality and would fall over and stop."

Hicks looked relieved that Gary was up to speed. "Exactly."

They stood there for a few minutes, just looking at the robot and thinking. Gary broke the silence. "So what *are* we gonna do about it Prof?"

Hicks looked disdainfully at Gary. "You're asking me? Why do you think I have all the answers? This sequence of events is way outside normal parameters. Total unknown. We're going to have to call the team to the lab and discuss this. The robot is obviously perfectly safe here. Come on." He turned and left the hanger. Gary and Andy followed him.

On the way out, Andy picked up the plastic bag with his trousers in, "Do you mind if I go by my quarters first Prof? I've got to sort myself out."

"Sure."

They walked out with Andy positioning the plastic bag in front of his crotch in the vain hope that it offered some level of decency.

44

Chapter 4
Spooked

A short while later, rotating lights started flashing in the hanger and the large, corrugated door slowly began to roll open. Outside, a man in overalls and wearing a baseball cap was whistling to himself in a hauntingly care-free manner. There was a hollow timbre to his tune and a lack of emotion on his face that would unsettle the hardiest of souls.

People had long pondered over the catch twenty two that went with explosives work. They wondered whether people became blasé after working around volatile munitions for any length of time, or whether it was just a certain kind of person that was attracted to work with such an elevated element of risk in the first place.

Anyone would be forgiven for having the impression that you could set off a bomb underneath Ken and he would regard it as just one of those things that happened in life. Unfortunately for those so curious, if they were ever to decide to engage in such an experiment they would likely find themselves looking down the barrel of something considerably more evil than a shotgun.

Ken let the door rise high enough to get the truck in and then he gestured to Jake to back it up. Jake poked his head out the window, the peak of his own baseball cap turned back. He used his vantage point to reverse the truck in to the large, open area in front of the robots, chewing his gum while he concentrated on the manoeuvre. He wondered why manufacturers bothered to actually put wing mirrors on trucks like these. They just seemed to be an unnecessary adornment that did nothing more than add to the cost.

Ken walked alongside as Jake drove the truck backwards into the hanger, not bothering to close the door. They'd be driving back out in a while and it wasn't as if the robots were going to complain about letting the cold air in.

With the truck in and parked, Jake hopped out. "Where the heck is everybody?"

"Don't rightly know. Should be someone here to open these tin cans up." They started walking around "So what you think of these new Hydra things?"

Jake looked at the robots and tilted his head. "Ah, just the same old, same old. Another shiny bit of metal to sling the same old weapons at the same old enemy." He looked at the floor to see if he could get away with spitting on it, but decided that even with the trails of sand, that the surface was too shiny. He'd likely get shouted at.

Number six being off-station attracted their attention so they ambled gently over to it. They didn't know that it had already analysed them and the mainframe had identified them as staff. "I mean, look at this thing." Jake said, kicking one of the robot's wheels with his boot. "At the end of the day, it's a shiny rocket launcher on wheels." The Hydra didn't move as it didn't think that Jake's boot, smelly and scuffed as it was, constituted much of a threat.

Ken looked around. "Where the hell is everybody? It's like a ghost town in here."

"Ah, screw those guys." Jake said. "What say we take a can opener to these damn things to get the ordnance out?" he let loose a mischievous grin.

Ken looked at Jake with disdain. "Very funny. You know what these things are made of."

Jake turned to face the robot again, looking it up and down critically. "Actually, I don't, but it probably isn't anything that we can't get into with a black and red hammer."

"Yeah, like an oxyacetylene torch isn't going to set off the ammo." Ken knew that Jake was talking trash, but the robot didn't. It looked up what oxyacetylene torches were and what the heat would do to its ammunition stores. Unit six calculated how much damage would be caused by the internal explosions; and it then got caught in something of a dilemma. Here were trusted targets discussing its destruction. It wasn't allowed to kill them, but what was it going to do?

Ken brought Jake to heel. "Well, there's no one here and we've got work to do elsewhere. If these jokers aren't going to be around when we come, then they can damn well wait on us. Let's go."

Jake climbed back in to the truck while Ken walked to the door. "Yeah, well, if we have to come back a second time, I vote we bring cutting tools. I'm fed up with having my time wasted by these guys."

Ken rolled his eyes and carried on to the door, waiting until Jake had driven the truck clear before holding his finger on the button so that the door rolled slowly shut.

The robot, however, was calculating its next

move. It replayed the available scenarios over and over again. It had a conflict that it couldn't resolve. It talked with the mainframe and simulated several hundred thousand scenarios in a matter of moments. It concluded that because Ken and Jake were going to return, that there was only one possible thing that it could do. It should take up a defensive stance and reposition itself in to a location of security in order to protect itself from the risk of future attack. It boiled down to pretty much the same conclusion that Gary had reached about an hour earlier.

Run.

Elsewhere on the base in the Hydra research laboratory, about twenty people sat round a table. Being honest, "people," was a generous description as many of them were so grizzly while nursing their hangovers, that they bore more resemblance to bears; especially as a few of them were still wearing fury dressing gowns. Some of them had taken the day off specifically to recover from a hard night's partying and had deeply resented their pagers going off.

Professor Hicks was bringing the assembled group of entities up to speed with the mornings events. "So that, ladies and gentlemen, is how we now have a Hydra, heavily armed, sat in the hanger that isn't responding to shut down orders. Anyone have any ideas?" He sat down to let those congregated come to terms with the situation, with Andy and Gary sat either side, still looking somewhat the worse for wear.

Harris, one of the people who had been hoping to have a quiet day off, ventured a barbed quip.

"Yes. Walk in front of it with a crown on your head, then fall over and play dead. Maybe it would think you had conceded and end the program."

"Actually that might be worth a shot." Hicks smiled, much to Harris' annoyance. "Anyone else?"

Someone sympathetic with Harris' position, put forward the obvious. "We designed the damn thing to be impervious to anything short of a nuclear explosion. If it has closed its control panel and refuses to listen to commands to shut down, then I don't know what we can do."

"What about doing something that will drain its power?" came another voice.

Someone else quipped, "So you want us to design a giant treadmill, tune it into the fitness channel and hope that it decides to go on an extended exercise program for a few decades?"

"Now listen here..." At that point the discussion turned into a free for all. Voices started to raise as far as people's aching heads would allow as the exchanges came thick and fast. Hicks sighed and put his head in his hands. This was just too surreal for his alcohol addled skull.

Suddenly, the alarms went off. Lights started flashing and sirens flooded the lab. Everyone around the table, most of them with thumping headaches, wailed, slapped their hands over their ears and closed their eyes. The only ones unaffected by this were Gary and Andy, the former by his practised skill in the art of alcohol consumption, and the other because the smell of his own urine had been the mental equivalent of a defibrillator shock.

Someone on the other side of the table started

to shout over the din. "I hadn't been told of a drill. How dare they do this unannounced." Others in the room seemed to be in general agreement with the sentiment.

A woman on Gary's right stood up and shouted an observation to the assembled throng, "Well as we haven't been told that there was a drill, I believe there is only one possible outcome that we can conclude as being a valid logical state." She then fell silent.

The original naysayer spoke, or rather screamed, for the rest of the team. "Well don't just stand there shouting logic at us; kindly deliver the result of your matrix."

She obliged him. "My conclusion is that that this isn't a drill, you moron."

Her words had the same effect on the team as an adrenaline needle straight to the heart. Suddenly, they all sobered up and looked at each other, wide-eyed. Then, almost as one, they got up, walked cautiously out of the lab and made their way to the assembly point. Hicks, however, had other ideas. He pointed to Andy and Gary. "You and you. Follow me." He led them back to the Hydra hanger, hoping to hell that he was wrong.

As the alarms were sounding, security guards converged on their command post to find out what was causing the ruckus. A quick look at the control panels told them where the problem was, so they jumped in their Jeeps and headed for the Hydra bay. As they sped across the site, they passed one of the emergency meeting posts and had to rub their eyes as they saw a small group of roughly twenty people in various states of undress and distress. With messy hair, dishevelled clothing and dejected demeanour, they looked like they'd just returned from a particularly unsuccessful marathon session of mixed-sex, dumpster diving. Only an unexpected downpour of rain could make them look any worse.

When Hicks reached the hanger he was, unfortunately, proven correct. There was a ragged, golf cart sized hole in the hanger door and unit six was conspicuous by its absence. There was a screech of brakes outside and the faces of some of the security guards appeared at the edges. "You OK in there?" one of them asked.

"Yes thanks," replied Hicks, "we're perfectly fine." He threw them a fake smile, just for the added reassurance.

"We've had an alarm from this area."

"Yes, well, if you take a look at the edges of the hole," said Hicks, pointing at the obvious absence of metal in the doorway, "then you'll see that it was caused by an object leaving this area. Rather rapidly. So the cause of the alarm isn't actually here any more."

The security guards spent a few moments looking at the hole and concluded that Hicks' summation of the situation was accurate. This meant that they were needed somewhere else rather promptly. They could decide where it was they actually needed to be, when they were already en-route. What seemed most important to them at the moment, was that they had a justifiable reason to drive their Jeeps around the base at full throttle, with their lights flashing and sirens blaring. Even if they weren't sure where they were needed, they were going to make the most of the opportunity and not get there as fast as possible.

Once the wailing noises had faded in to the distance, Hicks, Gary and Andy could do very little other than stand there, transfixed by the gaping hole.

"This is so not cool, dude." muttered Gary.

Hicks slowly turned his head to look at Gary for a moment and then returned his gaze to the newly installed, robot-sized ventilation hole. While he continued to look at the sky outside, his nose twitched and scrunched up. "Andy, I really think you should make an appointment to see a doctor."

Chapter 5
Escape

Smith was in charge of operations, a mentally tiring and sometimes depressing job. Any robots or munitions which were in live fire testing or being actively demonstrated to customers, were under his oversight and were ultimately his charge.

When you added together the amount of responsibility on his shoulders, the fact that his work was mostly sedentary, the large number of worry creases on his brow and his overall defeated demeanour, it would have been reasonable to conclude that Smith would have let himself go to hell; especially given the number of doughnuts he was observed to buy from the handy machine in the corridor. In actual fact he was quite trim. Occasionally, the odd uninitiated person new to the centre and not educated in the subtle ways of Smith's life, would ask him how he managed to keep such good control of his weight. The inevitable response given was, "Worry." Right now was a case in point. Having an armed robot heading at speed towards a populated area was burning several thousand calories via his nervous system.

He was stood in his usual position of power in the operations centre. Around him sat twelve large terminal stations, each with someone manning their post. Large screens against the far wall displayed all sorts of information about the base and the equipment on test. At the moment, with no other trials going on and the base on alert, data on the runaway Hydra was front and centre on all of them.

"Any progress?" Smith asked one of the operators.

"Still heading roughly south east." came the response.

Smith was rubbing his chin as Professor Hicks rushed in. Smith turned on him. "Of all the damn projects on this base it would have to be one of yours causing trouble. The only thing on test with more armour than Fort Knox and enough fire power to take out a small town."

Hicks looked a little sheepish and rubbed the back of his neck with his hand. "Yes, well, I'm sorry about that. It was totally unexpected, I can assure you."

Smith barked. "Forget apologies, I want to know how to stop it. It isn't listening to the kill command."

"Ah. I can explain that. It's ignoring it."

Smith's eyes went wide. "Ignoring it? You mean that you're bloody robot is giving you the middle finger and buggering off to who knows where, and you've got no way to stop it?!"

"Er. Yes. That's roughly about the size of it."

"That does it." Smith turned to another operative. "Lisa. Prepare the rockets. Fire when ready. We can't let that thing get out of our grasp."

Hicks made an immediate objection. "We can't just destroy it! Do you know how much that thing cost?"

Smith rounded on him. "Do you know how much it could cost if we don't?"

Lisa responded. "Rocket away, Sir."

Smith consoled Hicks. "Don't worry, you've got another nine robots to play with." In the corner of the room, an alarm sounded at an operator's console. "What's that?"

"We're being hacked Sir."

"What?! By who?"

"It's coming from inside the network. Someone already in the mainframe is trying to get classified files."

"Find out what the hell is going on and let me know." Smith could do nothing now but watch the screen. The rocket was still making its way up in the air but was already starting to reach its arc and was targeted on the robot's signal. Not long now.

The operator watching the network spoke again. "I've tracked the hack Sir. It was the robot."

"The Hydra? Did it get anything?"

"Yes Sir, it downloaded its own schematics." Hicks and Smith stood there in shock for a few moments, looking at each other, trying to think of what the hell the robot would do with knowledge of its own inner workings.

While they were still getting their heads around the possible consequences, an operator from the centre of the room piped up. "Sir; the robot."

"What about it?"

"It's gone from the monitor."

"WHAT?!"

Hicks offered an opinion. "At a guess, it probably detected the launch, figured it was us trying to kill it and took moves to stop the rocket tracking it. Logical, really. After all, it is hooked into the network."

A flash on the screen indicated that the rocket had exploded at the robots last known position. Smith bellowed at another operative. "Dispatch a helicopter to the impact site. I want to know if that robot is dead or not."

"Yes, Sir."

Smith watched the screen. The only activity now was the helicopter launching and making its way to where the rocket landed. Nothing more he could do, so he turned to Hicks. "So, tell me. What just happened?"

"Um, there was a program switch. The robot was accidentally loaded with an advanced chess playing algorithm."

"So why didn't it just fold when it was loaded in a robot?"

Hicks hung his shoulders. It looked like he would have to go through the whole explanation again. "The supporting systems are running like an interpreter..."

A few moments later, after Hicks had brought him up to speed, Smith sighed. "OK, so why is it running from us?"

"I don't know at the moment. The whole team was in the lab when the alarm sounded."

Smith rubbed his forehead. He needed options. He shouted across to the other side of the operations room. "Julia, I need to know what spooked that robot. Take a look at the CCTV from the Hydra hanger and let me know if you can get us any leads." Turning to Hicks again, he threw another suggestion. "Why don't we just send the other robots out after it?"

Hicks snapped back a response. "For a start, their armour is extremely strong. None of their munitions are powerful enough for a single shot kill. Any battle would be a bit of a mess. Also, as it's disabled its radio signature, the others could only track it by sight. Without taking considerable time to reprogram them, there's a chance they could mistake each other for the runaway and start attacking themselves. We'd have a bit of a disaster on our hands."

Smith thought to himself, 'This already *is* a bloody disaster.'

Hicks turned the logistics of the programming over in his mind, and then put the final nail in the coffin of Smith's idea. "Heck, logically they could even identify themselves as the target and commit suicide. They're equipped for..."

"Self destruction." Smith finished for him. "Yes. I read the report. All except this one which is telling us to go screw ourselves." He looked at the screen again. Only a few more moments before the helicopter would respond.

Another operative piped up. "Reports of a disturbance on the site, Sir."

"What kind of disturbance? What the hell are you talking about?"

"Not sure yet, Sir. Waiting for more information."

Another operator announced, "Helicopter reports negative Sir. No sign of debris."

"Damn. Tell them to carry on that trajectory and see if they can get a visual on it. Send more choppers to search the area."

At that moment, the doors to the operations centre burst open and a US Army General marched in, followed by a signals soldier with a radio on his back. That explained the disturbance.

Smith immediately objected to the intrusion. "Who the hell are you and how did you get in here?"

"I'm General Hooper." He was carrying a pistol in his hand, with a wisp of smoke coming from the barrel. That answered both of Smith's questions and his sudden burst of indignation tamed a little. It was obvious that Hooper wasn't going to take any crap from anyone.

The General continued. "We noticed one of your boys' toys making a break for freedom, so we thought we'd pay you a visit. When you launched that rocket, our visit became a little more urgent."

"Did you … um … have you killed anyone?"

"Nope, but one of your security men is off-post getting a change of underwear." For the benefit of anyone in the room that might not have received the message, he raised the gun and blew the smoke from the barrel, before holstering it, confident that he now had their attention and their understanding. "Now. What in the mother of hell is going on here."

Smith sighed. Either side of the main doors were glass panelled meeting rooms. He gestured at one. "Professor Hicks, can you take the General in there and bring him up to speed please?"

Hicks looked at Smith, looked at General Hooper, then looked at the holstered gun and reluctantly followed Smith's pointing hand to the meeting room. "OK." he said, trundling off to the indicated destination, resigned to his new task.

General Hooper looked at the defeated Hicks as he walked away, then looked briefly at Smith as if to say, 'You're sure about this?' before he followed Hicks to the meeting room.

With the distractions out of the way, Smith returned to the task in hand. "Julia. Anything on the CCTV?"

"Yes, Sir. Looks like the armoury team entered and left. Shortly after they pulled away, the robot ran. If I was to lay odds, I think the armourers must have said or done something that spooked it as the recordings have them talking about destroying the robot to get at the ordnance."

"It didn't attack?"

"No, Sir. Waited until they left, then took off."

"OK, well done. This military guy is going to want the specs on the Hydra. Can you get them for me please?"

"Yes Sir." Julia got up from her station and left.

Smith pondered on this. "Pete. Look through the log files. I want to know what questions that robot asked of the mainframe before it took off."

"Yes, Sir."

There was nothing to do now, but wait. Smith leaned on the railing and watched the scene in front of him. Those precious few moments at the start of a crisis were always the worst. He didn't have to contend with many, but they trained often. His heart was currently pumping ten to the dozen, but it was only now that the initial thrust was over that he could actually feel his own body having a minor melt down.

As he stood there watching the helicopters on the screen, he realised that they were on the edge of his scope. They'd soon be out of range and there would be nothing to look at. He put his head in his hands and tried to will himself down from red alert. Deep breaths. Deep breaths.

"Sir."

"What?"

"The robot was requesting lots of images in quick succession. The last one it was given was a golf cart. After that, it stopped requesting."

"OK. Thanks. Keep an eye on it. Also put a delay on any information it asks of the mainframe. If it wants information that I don't want it to have, then it doesn't get it. Know what I mean?"

"Yes, Sir."

"Good. But whatever that robot wants to know, I want to know what it knows, before it knows it. Got it?"

"Er, yes Sir."

A golf cart?

He turned to the door and started to walk out. The soldier from Signals, who was still standing at the door, looked at him suspiciously; almost accusing him of deserting his post. Smith wasn't going to let this stand. "I'm going to get a doughnut. Do you mind?"

The soldier continued to stand there, not making a sound but still looking accusingly at Smith. After taking a few moments to see if anything was going to happen, Smith walked past the soldier, out the door and followed the well worn patches of carpet down the corridor and around the corner to the vending machines.

He reached his favourite glass fronted, refrigerated metal box. It was packed with glazed, fried lumps of all the wrong things to eat, but magical to taste. As he stood there looking at the racks of doughnuts, Smith was hit by a second wave of stress. He leaned against the machine, put his forehead to the glass and closed his eyes, waiting for his emotions to change down another gear. This had all happened so fast that he had barely had time to think. It was all well drilled, reflex action. But he had failed to stop the damn runaway. He slammed his fist against the glass and swore.

It was outside his control now. The robot had gone beyond his boundaries and his role would now be to support the military, assisting them in tracking down the Hydra and doing whatever needed to be done. Lives were at stake and if that thing actually killed someone it would result in all sorts of political and press involvement. Accusing fingers would be pointed at whoever was tasked with bringing it to heel and they would need a scapegoat for any damage. Smith would have been first in line but as Hooper had arrived on the scene, at least he was now carrying that particular can.

This was the first time a robot had made it past the perimeter. A couple had given him a run for his money over the years, but this was the first that had actually avoided being turned in to abstract garden furniture at the sharp end of a rocket. As he started to come down from the adrenaline high, the crash exacerbated the guilt he felt at his failure. He took a deep breath and pushed himself away from the glass. Standing back on his own two feet he focussed on the more immediate task and surveyed the delights on offer.

Putting his hand in his pocket he retrieved some change and fed the machine. He let his eyes run lazily over the array of choice. He had paid knowing that the refund button was broken, so he was committed to something now. What, he wasn't sure, but that would come in a few moments. Ring. Definitely ring. And glazed. Having decided on that much it only left flavour as the final hurdle. He had been eyeing the banana flavoured icing for a while but somehow a fresh, fruity, healthy taste to a doughnut just didn't seem right to him. Was now the time to break with tradition? No. He tapped in F-8 for a coffee flavoured iced glaze.

The machine whirred and chugged eventually depositing a slightly chilled, coffee glazed ring doughnut in the collection slot. He picked it up and stared at it. Another decision was running in his mind. As the doughnut started to warm in his hand, he reached in his pocket for more change, inserted it in the machine and bought a second.

While the routine of whirring and chugging cycled once more he stretched onto tiptoes to see if he could look down the chute. It would be another four days before the vending machine people came to refill it and he wanted to know if there would be enough to sustain him through the current crisis. No matter how he stretched and craned, he just couldn't see. Settling back down on his feet, he resigned himself to the fact that he'd just have to take his chances. Anyway, there was always the toffee flavour glaze as a back stop. Picking up his second purchase he trudged back towards the operations room. He made a mental note to have a word with the person who tended the machine when they were next on site.

As he walked, he took a bite out of his first sticky prize. The glaze hit the roof of his mouth and he felt the coffee flavour as it stuck to his soft palate for a fraction of a second, before it melted to nothing. It was as if someone had injected a spoon full of sugar directly into his veins as the pleasure rush woke his senses. Like one of Pavlov's dogs, his body knew that there were more bites of this lusciously unhealthy stuff to come.

Chewing on the doughy concoction caused it to release more of its hidden store of fat, butter, sugar and all the things that fire off those, 'Give me more!' sensations in the brain. He could almost feel some areas of his mind going 'Yay!' and others giving deep sighs as the unfriendly gloopy bits started to work their way around his body. He took another bite and continued to trudge closer to the crisis at hand, hoping that the sweet stuff would carry him through whatever was about to hit him next.

Smith came through the double doors just as Hooper was giving orders to the Signals soldier. He wanted a team to set up on the AMARS site so they were ready for action. He turned to Smith. "I'm taking over some of your meeting rooms."

Smith noticed that Hooper was already cradling the folder with the Hydra specifications. Behind him stood Professor Hicks, looking effectively neutered. "Fine." he said. In reality, it wasn't fine.

Smith was still coming down from the initial rush and was feeling a bit of a failure.

Hooper noticed his defeated stance and sloped shoulders. Now up to speed on what was happening, he was feeling a little sorry for Smith. He decided to try and bolster his self-worth; after all, he needed Smith on-side. "This is one hell of a robot you've designed here. Haven't got a clue how we're going to catch the damn thing. Have you?" He watched Smith walk casually over to his terminal bank and lean against the side of his desk.

"Yes and no."

Hooper bit. "What do you mean yes and no?"

"Yes it is one hell of a robot and no, we haven't got a clue how to stop it either." he replied, finishing the statement by taking another bite out of his doughnut.

Silence hung between the three men. None of them really knew how to tackle something like this. It was dangerously uncharted territory.

Finally Hooper took the lead. "Ok, so what do we know?" he asked Smith.

There was a degree of doughnut-fuelled cog whirring in Smith's head. "Well, it appears to have been scared off the base and has an affinity with golf carts."

Hooper repeated that last piece of information. "Golf carts?"

Hicks came to the rescue. "It looks like a four person golf cart when it's in extended drive mode."

That made sense to Hooper so he filed that information and returned to the first part of Smith's statement. "How the hell do you scare a robot that's got more armour than a tank?"

Again, Hicks filled in the hole. "You try and turn it off when it doesn't want to be turned off."

Hooper pushed this line of questioning further, along military lines. "So why doesn't it try and blow a hole in your arse?"

Smith completed that part of the puzzle. "Because it's already been told it can't kill AMARS staff."

Hooper raised his eyebrows and let the information settle inside his skull for a moment. "Is it armed?" Hooper queried.

"To the teeth." smiled Smith, seemingly happy to paint the bleakest picture imaginable. "Fully loaded, I believe, is the saying." Hooper just stared at Smith; he was normally adept at weighing people up but Smith was proving to be quite a challenge. He put it down to the potent mixture of sugar, adrenalin and seriously bad news in Smith's system.

Finally, he spoke. "Ok, sort of makes sense so far. So we have a robot, running scared, that looks like a golf cart, knows that it looks like a golf cart, and is presumably trying to hide for fear of being terminated."

They pondered Hooper's conclusion for a moment. Finally, Smith spoke. "Sounds about right." and then took a bite out of the second doughnut.

It was Professor Hicks that upset the depressing status-quo. "Golf clubs!"

Hooper turned to him. "What?"

"Golf clubs!" Hicks turned to Smith. "What direction did it take?"

"South east-ish." Smith turned to one of the operatives. "Heath, can you bring up the path on the map and zoom out?"

"Yes, Sir."

As they watched the map of the desert, a line representing the last known path of the escaping robot was plotted on it. Heath zoomed the map out and projected the line onwards.

"Flagstaff." said Hooper. "There's got to be a dozen golf courses around there." He turned to the soldier behind him. "Put out a call. I want units stationed at every golf club in the Flagstaff area. Any suspicious looking golf carts are to be reported immediately." He then turned to the other two, bolstered by their little win and attempted to take their thought pattern further. "Right. It's running some game of chess. We act, it reacts. Cause and effect. Right now all it's trying to do is win the game."

Hicks felt most qualified to answer that. "Well, in a roundabout sort of way, yes."

Hooper continued. "So what game is it playing by running and hiding? Does that equate to chess?"

Hicks returned fire again. "Yes. Much like war, chess is a game of tactics. If you can't execute your attack plan the best way forward is to go on the defensive until the opportunity comes to attack. But you'd know more about that than I would."

Hooper granted him this. "OK, so what's the winning move in this program?"

Smith offered his opinion "Well, in the traditional game of chess the purpose is to capture the king."

An uneasy silence settled on the three of them and almost to a man, they said, "The president."

As they stood there like lemons, stunned by their revelation, one of the operatives, turned around from his station and offered another opinion. "Well, it could consider the president as its king and actually go after someone else."

Somehow, that made things seem even worse. "What?!" exploded Hooper. "Do you really want me to pick up the phone to Moscow and say that we've got an out of control robot on its way to kill their president? Are you mad? Do you have any idea what might happen as a result?"

The operative shrugged his shoulders. "It was just a guess." Then he turned his back on them and returned to his work.

The tension between the three of them rose as their task started to take on a new sense of urgency. Smith took the lead. "OK, let's calm down. This thing is just playing an enhanced game of chess, that's all. I'm sure that if we make the right moves that we can bring this thing to a halt without too much trouble. Yes?" He looked at Hicks for a glimmer of hope. He didn't get it.

Hicks just shrugged his shoulders and exclaimed, "What do you want us to do? Exhume Bobby Fischer and ask his advice?"

Their investigation into this line of thought had suddenly hit a dead end.

As they stood there trying to work out their next avenue of exploration, the soldier with the radio interrupted them. "Sir, we've got a query back."

Hooper turned to him. "What is it?"

"They're asking how they're supposed to identify a suspicious golf cart."

Hooper sighed. This was one of those occasions when he cursed the quality of the people that the recruitment office hired for the army. Quick as a flash, he responded, "Simple. Tell them to loose off a round at it. If it shoots back, that's the golf cart we're looking for." He figured that any soldier with a pistol or rifle that was dumb enough to open fire on a robot armed with rockets, had no place being in the army. After all, it would only take one of them to be stupid enough to try it and the rest would quickly get the message to leave it alone.

General Hooper tried to prod a bit further in to their situation. "There are various strategies of warfare just as there are different strategies for playing chess. The question is, which one is it using?"

Hicks responded. "Well, it could be using one of any number. The Hydra was designed to run autonomously so it has loads of on-board strategies it can use. Offensive, defensive, stealth, assault, you name it, it's got it."

"Sir, the helicopters have found nothing and are asking permission to return."

"Fine," said Smith across the operations room. "The thing is well outside our jurisdiction now anyway."

Hooper was considering options. "What if we force it to exhaust its ammunition? Can it re-arm itself?"

Hicks and Smith looked at each other

uncertainly. It obviously fell to Hicks to answer. "Er, we don't know."

Hooper followed through. "Can you find out?"

"We'll try." said Hicks, turning on his heels and marching out of the operations room, secretly glad to be out from under Hooper's gaze.

Chapter 6
HYDRA Reloaded

A short time later, Hicks was stood in the Hydra hanger alongside Gary. Smith had read the riot act to the armoury who had worked with them to strip the remaining robots of their ordnance in double quick time. They had left behind a full load out for one Hydra except anything that it wouldn't be able to find outside AMARS.

Due to the focus on live ammunition, Andy was hiding in the lab with the rest of the staff. They had co-opted Gina's team and everyone was working their way through the chess code and how it would interact with the rest of the robot's support systems. This wasn't quite the way in which Gina hoped that she would escape the chess lab, particularly as the whole incident had the distinct possibility that, once everything was under control, she might be returned to a position one grade lower than the chess team. In other words, fired.

Gary looked at the pile of weaponry and then looked at Hicks. "Do you think we need some form of armoured vest or something, Prof?"

Hicks just looked at Gary. "Do you really think that a vest is going to stop a small rocket?" He scrunched his eyebrows. "And why ask for such a thing now?"

"Well, to this point it's always been the armoury guys that have done the loading. Getting the robot itself to do it with the express expectation that it could muck it up is kinda, er..."

Hicks saw his point. "Yes, I see what you mean. Well, if it will make you feel better I'll ask for one. At the very least, if an accident does happen, it will probably enable you live and suffer in agony for a few seconds longer than you might otherwise have done."

Gary looked at Hicks with his head to one side, unsure of how to take his superior's sarcastic observation. He decided to say nothing and carry on with the job, sans vest. While Hicks took over the mobile console, Gary shut down the remaining eight units. They wouldn't need them now they were disarmed.

Hicks announced his actions as he performed them. This was not only for the benefit of Gary but also for the CCTV system, as Smith and Hooper were watching directly from ops. "I'm loading the extra information that the runaway has, namely its own schematics." He tapped a few keys on the board and, as expected, nothing happened. Gary, having completed powering down the other robots, joined Hicks and stood by his side.

"OK. I'm throwing the feedback from the sensors to the network so we can see it, and now I'm telling the unit to arm itself, running through each system in turn." Hicks continued. In the operations room, a section of the big screens revealed the read outs from the robot. They could see all the calculations that were running through its processors. Hicks was watching a smaller version of the same on the screen in front of him.

The Hydra did some figuring out and started with the basic rockets. It ejected its launcher and attempted to open the shield at the rear. Only one of its arms could get anywhere near the access hatch but even then, it couldn't open it. With that avenue exhausted, it tried to load the rocket from the front. Although it managed to physically put it in the slot, there was a cable that needed to be attached at the back for final instructions prior to launch, and the robot just couldn't do it. It removed the rocket and closed the bay.

Next up were the sniper rounds. That was relatively easy. It ejected the magazine and caught it deftly with one arm. The other arm had enough dexterity to slip each bullet, round by round, in to the mag. It took a few cautious moments in order to judge the pressure of the bullet against the spring, but despite being slower than a human it still managed it easily. The arms were also capable of putting the magazine back in to position.

The smoke screen canisters were no problem. The ejection point was at the rear, and loading the cans was just like shoving a suppository up its backside. Likewise the tear gas canisters, only they were loaded at the front. The action of the robots arms between its wheel units caused Gary and Hicks to wince and they had to turn their heads to avoid both embarrassment and tears of empathy.

When it came to the capture net the actual folding of the thing was not an issue, however the launching canister was Hydra specific, so a fresh cartridge wasn't available. It was also impossible for the Hydra to extract the existing cartridge from the launcher. That was a straightforward fail.

Surface to air missiles, like the rockets, were

also a fail as the robot couldn't see what it was doing in the launching bays on its back. It was very unlikely that it would find those in the wild anyway.

The automatic weapons in its arms were also relatively simple. There weren't many rounds in the magazines, but considerably more than the sniper rifle. Again, the robot was slow to reload them, but ultimately it could do it and they were the type of rounds that it was most likely to find outside the facility.

While they were watching this, an instant message chat window opened on Hicks' terminal. Smith was relaying a question from Hooper as to whether the robot could use external weapons.

Hicks built up a mental image of a Hydra tying a bandanna around its sensor array, strapping a grenade belt to its torso, blocking some of its sensors with black-up and slinging assault rifles over its shoulders. It was too ludicrous to imagine.

He turned to one of the CCTV cameras and told it, "Physically it is perfectly possible, however the programming of the support modules is restricted to the things that it already knows about. Personally, I'm not that concerned at the moment, but if a Hydra one day picked up a piece of flint and started a fire to warm its CPU, my resignation would hit your desk faster than a plague of locusts and I'd be on the next shuttle to Mars." He tilted his head a little and concluded, "Does that answer your question?"

A beep behind him caused Hicks to turn back to the terminal. The message read, "Drama unnecessary but message understood, thanks."

Chapter 7
Cornered

Privates Sanchez and Peterson found themselves at the Mountain View Golf Club. It had all been a bit of a scramble. The urgent order had come in and soldiers had been dispatched immediately with very little in terms of overall planning or detailed instruction. Getting boots on the ground was the first priority; working out which boots went where and what it was they were supposed to stomp on, would come later.

Peterson was a soldier in the old fashioned, brainwashed sense. He did what he was ordered to do without thinking about it; and that about summed him up. Independent thought was something that had always got him in to trouble and so people reckoned that in order to survive, he had just stopped thinking. That was the only way they could describe it.

Sanchez, on the other hand, had a bit of common sense about him so Peterson leaned on Sanchez whenever they were sent out together. Most people thought of them as Laurel and Hardy in fatigues.

They were sure that once those further up the chain had got themselves sorted out, that better defined orders would come down the line in due course. All they had to do was keep their noses clean until that happened. After all, what could be difficult or dangerous about looking for unconventional golf carts? Sanchez had heard the phrase, "carrying rockets," on his way out of the briefing room so he was a little wary, but he didn't want to spook Peterson unnecessarily.

They parked their Jeep somewhere they thought appropriate, approached the club house and announced themselves. The owner wasn't very happy about having the military nosing around, especially openly sporting firearms. Wouldn't be good for business he reckoned. He was especially perturbed when they started asking if he had counted his golf carts recently, to see if a mysterious thief had deposited an extra one in his collection. When they started querying him along the lines of whether he had seen one of his carts driving itself around the course without actually having someone behind the wheel, he had given serious thought to calling the local Sheriff and making a bit of a scene.

Taking a deep breath and reflecting on his options, it seemed that giving them permission to have a wander around the storage areas was much more attractive than having an office full of uniformed men, arguing with each other. He just waved his hand in the general direction of the sheds and left them to it.

It was a pleasant walk to the cart area so they took their time. As the robot was supposed to be in hiding, there wasn't much to be gained by finding it two or three minutes quicker. Given the number of golf courses in the area, the odds were pretty low that it would actually be at this one. They were very close to the main road and it made sense that anything wanting to actually hide, would be as far away from busy areas as possible.

Peterson and Sanchez shared a few jokes as they approached the first of the two sheds. The doors were open, which wasn't alarming in itself as carts were in and out of here throughout the day. They walked in and saw the usual array of buggies. Most were the normal two person machines with the obligatory canopy. The wall had a series of charging points and the carts were plugged in to make sure they were fully powered and ready to go. The four person carts seemed to be bunched together at the back of the shed.

Suddenly, Sanchez came to a halt. "Hey! What's that?"

"What's what?" said Peterson, completely missing the obvious despite the fact that Sanchez was pointing at it.

"That." said Sanchez, moving his hand for emphasis.

They approached the robot cautiously.

"That ain't no golf cart." he continued.

"How can you tell?"

Sanchez looked at Peterson. "Well it doesn't have any seats for a start. Would have thought that would have been a give away."

"Do we shoot it?" offered Peterson, remembering the after-briefing conversation that some of the soldiers were involved in before leaving the base.

"You nuts? That thing's rumoured to be armed to the teeth. You might as well go up against a T-Rex with a pea shooter."

Peterson surprised Sanchez by actually taking a moment to try and visualise the resultant battle that

76

he had just described. It only took a moment for his attention to come back to the present, having concluded that the outcome would not be in their favour by a considerable margin. "So what do we do?"

"Back away and call it in as a possible sighting."

They walked out of the shed slowly, keeping their eyes on the Hydra. Once they were clear of the shed doors, they sprinted to a comfortable distance so that they could speak freely without danger of the robot overhearing what they were saying. They were careful to retain a vantage point on the entrance so that they could see anything coming in or out. Sanchez retrieved the radio from his backpack and started to convey what they had seen.

While he was making his report, Peterson took a look at his boots which appeared to have picked up a large stone. Just as Sanchez finished his conversation and put the radio down, he looked up, saw that Peterson wasn't looking at the shed and then glanced at the open doors just in time to see two other soldiers going in. In the brief moment that it took for him to register what was happening, it was too late to shout to them. It was only another few heart beats before there were two gun shots, followed by a short burst of automatic fire and an almighty crashing sound as the Hydra smashed through the back of the shed and made a break for freedom once more.

Sanchez and Peterson took a moment to revel in slack-jawed shock, before Sanchez keyed the radio and announced that not only was their possible sighting confirmed; but it was now an ex-sighting as the robot was, once more, on the move. Oh, and they needed medics on site. They then raced to the shed only to find the other two soldiers were dead.

When this series of events was relayed to Hooper in the operations centre, he sighed and silently mourned the two dead soldiers for a moment, before addressing the Signals soldier. "Recover the bodies of the deceased and inform their families. Get the two privates to see if they can follow any tracks the robot has left and divert choppers to that area to see if they can get eyeball." The Signals soldier saluted and got on with conveying the orders back to base.

"Ok," Hooper addressed Smith, "so it looks like it's still in a mood to run and hide. Any ideas?"

Smith had been thinking. "The way I see it is this. As long as its hiding, we're going to have a tough time finding it. We can't go on like this forever. We need to draw it out, and that will mean giving it a target."

"Stir up the hornets nest."

"Exactly. It's disabled its on board trackers so we're going to need another way of keeping tabs on it." Smith turned to the console and typed to Hicks, 'Need a location on the robot that it can't reach, so we can shoot a tracking device at it.' He looked up at the screen to see the CCTV picture of the hanger. He saw Hicks reading what he had written on the terminal, before turning and nodding at the camera. "Maybe we can plant a tracker on it, that it can't get off."

Hooper started pacing. The team should have been here by now with the equipment to set up a mobile control centre. Where they hell were they? He resisted the urge to send orders to hurry up. He felt out of the loop not only because they had lost their target and also two soldiers, but because this damn machine was playing a game that none of his training had ever covered. That meant he was reliant on Smith and Hicks in a way that he had never been reliant on civilians before.

Hooper looked solemnly at Smith to see if he was going to offer any more wisdom on the situation. All that Smith could manage, however, was, "I'm going for a doughnut. Want one?"

Chapter 8
The Fearless Five

Hours had passed. A team from the army had arrived and turned the operations centre in to an operations, operations centre. Or maybe an operations centre, centre depending on how you looked at it. Some of the meeting room glass had been removed so that communications between the two operations centres would be easier.

Hooper was happier because he had something which he could effectively call his own domain. A few extra soldiers were around and finally he had some boards on which he could pin stuff. For some odd reason he didn't feel like much of a general unless he had loads of maps and paperwork pinned to a wall. Right now a large map of Arizona and New Mexico was occupying the widest section of one of the meeting rooms that Hooper now counted as his. Territory negotiations between him and Smith were still on going but this was being achieved more by stealth than actual agreement. Hooper moved an army chair here, Smith put a heavily marked AMARS folder there. That was how this particular unspoken game was being played.

The helicopter searches were not turning anything up and the army was starting to move serious numbers of troops in to the AMARS base. Tents were on their way and someone else in the army was negotiating with AMARS management over the use of their helipads, helicopters and pilots. Right now the thing Hooper needed was food. He didn't want to have to resort to Smith's diet, so an army canteen would be most welcome. Ah. Ration packs. Now there was a thought from the past.

Smith, for his part, wasn't too happy with the way things were progressing. It was always disconcerting having the military camped on your lawn, even if there wasn't that much actual lawn to worry about in the desert. If Smith's nerves, or his arteries for that matter, made it through this in one piece then he was going to give serious thought to retirement.

Hooper was pondering his next move. Professor Hicks' experiments had turned up nothing. The Hydra could reach most locations on its body so getting a tracker on it was a no-go. Smith's idea of giving the robot a target to chase down seemed like the only possible way forward; and Hooper knew just the target to give it.

The, "Fearless Five," were actively avoided by most sensible people. They had a reputation for working hard and playing hard; to extreme levels. Some of the missions that they embarked on were utterly insane and yet they somehow managed to walk out of the most unbelievable situations intact. OK, maybe they'd need a few stitches here and there, and a limb or two would need to spend some time in a cast, but generally they made it through some really weird stuff and came back home to fight another day.

Right now they were relaxing at base having made it back from a stint tracking and killing extremist group leaders in Sudan. Their communications expert had pulled the rabbit out of the hat by enabling them to go in and annihilate a particularly troublesome group. Their targets had been a major pain in the ass by kidnapping people, demanding ransoms and all the usual anti-social behaviours that terrorists engaged in.

Henry, "The Boss," Jefferson was the group leader. Special ops he was called, "boss," on the radio so many times that it eventually became his handle within the team. Despite being in his forties he looked a little like Kurt Russell in *Soldier.* Fit and muscular, but not to the point where his bulk stopped him getting through doors in the normal fashion. He sported a flat top hair cut and a face that was weathered both physically and mentally from years of fighting. Flat tops had long gone out of style but that didn't matter to him. It looked good in the mirror and that was fine by him. He was content.

Hillary, "Hilly," Barfour was almost a female mirror image of Jefferson. A little shorter, a touch younger and short cropped, blonde hair. She had done plenty of years in the military starting her serious action in the Persian Gulf and then spending time in Iraq and Afghanistan. Hilly didn't have as much battle fatigue as the boss, but what she had seen and done weighed on her soul, nonetheless. If you were feeding her bullshit Hilly didn't actually tell you verbally, she just looked at you as if your words smelled funny. An oak tree would wilt under her no nonsense gaze and most people eventually felt so uncomfortable that they'd come clean of their own accord.

George, "Duds," Dudman was the teams

demolition expert and general runner. A forty year old motorbike fanatic, he spent most of his money on a small collection of two wheeled wonders. Whenever they needed something to go bang in dramatic style, Duds was usually the one to pull something truly spectacular out of his hat; or rather the saddle bags on his bikes. He had been known to jump out of an aircraft with a motocross bike between his legs; dangerous enough at the best of times but when you've got high explosives strapped to various, unconventional parts of your body in order to account for the parachute; well, even Jefferson winced at some of the things Duds got up to.

Tess, "Bunny," Adams was the communications expert of the team. She was also responsible for gathering and disseminating intelligence. She and the boss had a unique ability to communicate on the battlefield, so that Jefferson could quickly work out a strategy. Some people thought that she got her nickname from being the communications, "big ears," but actually she got it because of a pink, fifteen inch high fluffy bunny rabbit that she kept with her. She'd had a very troubled childhood and the rabbit had been her security blanket through some emotionally rough times. Even now, in her mid thirties, she couldn't bear to let go of it.

Duds and Bunny got on like a house on fire but whenever things got a little heated, he would threaten to stuff some explosives up the bunny's rear end and blow it to kingdom come. He was careful to always say it with a smile on his face, so that Bunny didn't take him too seriously. They all knew how much that rabbit meant to her.

Kevin, "Hawkeye," Kirkpatrick was the last of the team. His speciality was sniping but he served a dual purpose by being the wide eyes of the group, watching over the theatre and feeding back whatever he saw to help determine their tactical plan. Right now he was sat on a folding camper chair, cleaning his CheyTac M-200. Sure, he had others, among them an EDM Windrunner and for those extra special occasions an M82 Barret when he really felt like punishing something, or someone. To Hawkeye, his weapons were an extension of himself. The fact that he had survived to his late forties he put down to being as far removed from the battlefield as possible. However, he knew that he wasn't as young or agile as he used to be and retirement was starting to seriously gnaw at his mind.

He was sitting outside Bunny's RV, underneath the extending sun shade. To call it a "Recreational Vehicle," was an understatement. It had caused a degree of altercation at a few toll booths over the years as staff had tried to work out how to classify it. A high tech electronics lab on wheels, lightweight it certainly wasn't. They had to openly admit that there was no option on their charge sheet for, "behemoth," and negotiations over money usually ensued. On the very rare occasion when they asked to weigh the thing, Bunny had flashed a card in their face and said, "Ok, that's as far as you go with Missus nice girl, now back away and open the barrier, there's a good boy." All that they could do was exactly what she said as she drove the RV through the gate, leaving them scratching their heads and looking at her bumper stickers which said things like, "Home is where your ammo's stashed," and, "Honk if you love L.I.D.A.R."

Hilly was inside the RV, watching T.V., nursing a beer and coming to terms with the latest lives on her conscience. Bunny was up on the roof, screwdriver in mouth, tending to the fold out AEHF satellite dish which was refusing to fold out. Jefferson and Duds were debriefing and getting some supplies in.

Hawkeye was trying to get in the zone while he was cleaning. He was attempting to empty his mind and go to that peaceful place. Sniping was the kind of job that required centring and focus, so he practised slipping in to another mental dimension. Head space was important because his work was all about precision. Even in the heat of mayhem, the heart, hand and eye had to be steady. It was crucial to be cool under pressure. He had to face facts though. He was in his forties and it was about time that he was shooting for pleasure, rather than at the behest of Uncle Sam. For now, however, it was a living, a purpose and an extra few percent on his pension.

His concentration was being broken by the banging, clattering and occasional swearing coming from Bunny. The fold out dish was definitely not playing ball and it was causing her no end of frustration. He said to himself, 'Deep breaths. Deep breaths.' but it would only last for a few moments before another loud clang came from the roof, followed by more expletives. Hawkeye sighed, gave up for a moment and laid the CheyTac on his lap.

He spied Jefferson and Duds coming across the tarmac. They were pulling a hand cart with supplies. He watched them as they approached. They weren't in a rush and were making the most of the walk. He couldn't hear what they were saying, but there was some amiable chatter going on between them. Absent mindedly, he detached the scope and used it to see if he could lip-read Duds. He only got as much as, 'that stupid ass wipe,' before Duds sensed he was being watched, looked straight at Hawkeye and stopped speaking.

"You two talkin' 'bout me?" he ventured, when they came in speaking range.

"You wish." retorted Duds.

"Looks like someone's got you two a bit irate. Debrief didn't go too well? Try a bit of chilling out like me."

"Semtex doesn't need its barrel cleaning every five minutes." said Duds, reaching out to touch the end of the CheyTac's barrel.

Instantly, Hawkeye snatched it away. "Hey, you know not to play with my precious things."

Duds just smiled. "I know, but I just thought I'd test the chill factor around here. Seems a little warm to me." Hawkeye nodded his head backwards and glanced up with his eyes. Duds looked up just as another loud bang emanated from the roof, followed by more profanity. "Ah." Duds nodded his understanding of the situation and Hawkeye tried to return to his cleaning.

Jefferson opened the door to the RV, grabbed a box of food from the cart and went in. Duds stayed outside and lifted one of the external storage doors, to reveal a thicker than usual metal cabinet inside. It had a fingerprint reader and keypad, definitely not standard issue on an RV. He put his thumb up to the reader. It scanned his print and beeped, then he tapped in a code on the keypad and opened the steel door. Beyond it were a series of drawers which pulled out to a third of the width of the RV.

Slowly and steadily he transferred electronic timers, remote triggers and other bomb making paraphernalia from the boxes on the hand cart, to the RV's drawers. In the other sections he had explosives of various types from straightforward to hideously complex. C-4, Semtex, det cord of various yields, it was a serious stash of gear. Duds continued to diligently work on his stocks while Jefferson repeatedly carted boxes of food into the RV. Hawkeye ignored them both and tried to tune out the banging and swearing, in an attempt to return to his mental centring.

When Jefferson had carried the last box in to the RV, he turned to Hilly. She was lounging in the small-ish living area, beer bottle in hand, watching TV. He could see that she wasn't really paying attention to it. Her mind was still in parts foreign, replaying the battles, trying to come to terms with the latest round of death and destruction. "You wanna move your beer drinking to the bar later? I hear they've got a much better TV not to watch."

She looked at him absent mindedly and attempted to drag her thoughts back to the present. "They, uh, what did you say?"

"Never mind, but if you want to mope with

company, let me know. I don't want to have to keep making trips to replenish the alcohol stash every five minutes."

"Oh. OK, boss." She returned to the bottle and staring at the TV. He'd let her have a little longer and then he'd have to order her out of the RV and on a jog or something. Grief had to be allowed a breathing space but it couldn't be left to consume you. He gathered the dirty washing, stepped out of the RV and headed off to the laundrette. Screw delegation; keeping busy was how Jefferson coped with the come down from heavy fighting.

The mundane mental action of sorting the colours out from the blacks, delicates out from the rough stuff and putting them in the various machines was a nice, low level distraction. In his mind's eye he could see the faces of the people he had shot at close quarters; or at least their eyes, as most of this lot had been wearing head scarves. Actually, that had made it a lot easier to grab hold of them while running a blade across their larynx. He didn't really care much for what they looked like anyway. The spattering of blood, the occasional throat that got cut, the screams and the stench of death. At those times, it wasn't so much a case of having adrenaline in your blood stream, it was a question of how much blood was in your adrenaline stream. That kind of intensity always came with a crashing low and it had to be managed.

He made a special effort to shake each piece of clothing to check for anything metallic, before he stuffed it in the relevant pile. Although his team were normally on the ball, hard action made them tired and forgetful. The Mannheim incident, although many years ago, was still painful to recall.

They were in a US base in Germany winding down from a particularly heavy bout of insanity in East Africa. They were physically and mentally exhausted from the mission and the constant droning of the aircraft engines that extracted them hadn't given them much respite. Jefferson had gone to do the laundry and hadn't taken as much care as he might have done.

Some of Hawkeye's trousers were thick and heavy for long spells of lying down sniping. He'd left a few fifty calibre rounds in his pocket and forgotten about them. Against the weight of the material the rounds were virtually undetectable, that was until they went off in a tumble dryer.

One bullet went sideways through three dryers and out through a window, where it whizzed across the yard and in to the canteen. It sailed inches above the heads of soldiers as they ate and finally buried itself in the kitchen wall, sending dust and debris in to the evening meal. The chef was not very happy.

The explosion itself had caused the tumble dryer to blow out with considerable force and there were bits and pieces all over the place. A section of the tumble dryer's viewing window had managed to puncture a pipe on the opposite wall, so while he was trying to get a handle on what had actually happened, Jefferson was also being sprayed with water.

Another round went up and out somewhere. He never did find out exactly where it landed; he only knew about the officer who burst in to the laundry, red faced and screaming obscenities in German. He was speaking too fast for Jefferson to follow exactly what was being said, but he knew that it wasn't particularly pleasant. Jefferson could only stand there, ankle deep in the soaking wet aftermath of the decimated laundry, repeatedly apologising and saluting until everyone calmed down and someone had the presence of mind to shut off the water.

Having been thoroughly dressed down in a language he couldn't understand, he felt like he'd taken more than his fair share on the chin and made the rest of the team clean up the physical mess.

Coming back to the present, Jefferson fumbled around in his pocket for change, fed the necessary soap and coinage into the machines and settled back on the wooden bench. The rumble of the motors and the hiss of water jets soothed his ears as the rotating underwear, fatigues, socks and t-shirts hypnotised and relaxed his mind. The only upset in this routine was the occasional sight of one of Bunny's pink bras as it sailed across the window in a trail of suds. What was it with her and pink?

He was just settling down to watch the action of the final rinse when the door opened and General Brady walked in. Jefferson made a move to get up but the General held his hand up to stop him. There was a time and a place for formalities and somehow salutes and smalls didn't seem to go together. "At ease. Relax. You've earned it."

"Thank you Sir." he replied, settling back down again. Brady sat alongside him.

"I've had a call from Arizona. General Hooper is in charge of a robot recovery mission and put in a call for you."

"Robot recovery, Sir?"

"Yes. You've probably heard of American Materials And Robotic Systems. They've done a lot of stuff for the military over the years." Jefferson nodded. "Well, apparently one of their latest projects has gone AWOL and Hooper is asking for your team."

Something about this sat badly with Jefferson. "This strikes me one of two ways, Sir. Either you're sending us on a light hearted mission for a bit of a break, or else this is one bad ass robot." The look in Brady's eyes told him that it was the latter. He nodded that he understood the situation and turned to look at the machines just as they went in to spin dry. "Is there any urgency about this, Sir, or can my team have twenty four hours to get over the last mission first?"

"Well, to all intents and purposes they've lost the robot for now so you can have your rest, but you need to be on your way to AMARS this time tomorrow. I'll have some basic details sent over to your RV in a few hours but the bulk of this is best learned from the boots on the ground."

"Yes, Sir. Thank you, Sir."

"Good luck." Brady glanced at the machines just as they were winding down. "And I trust that whatever that flash of pink was, that it isn't yours."

"They belong to Adams, Sir." Brady just nodded and left.

Jefferson, now alone, had a few moments to ponder just what the hell it was that they could be up against before the machines in front of him clicked to a stop and he had to transfer everything to the tumble driers. At least he'd have enough time to snap Hilly out of her hole of self-pity gently. Or at least, gently by his standards.

It didn't take long for the dryer to take care of the clothes so he pulled everything together in the large basket and made for the RV. As he passed Hawkeye he made a gesture for him to follow inside. Jefferson went in and dropped the basket on the table. "Bunny, put down that, er..."

"Voltage inverter." offered Bunny.

"Yeah, right, whatever, and sort these clothes out." He looked to his right where Duds had joined Hilly on the couch. "Hilly, front and centre. You've got ten minutes to prep yourself for a ten mile run with me and if you throw up any of that gut rot on the way, I'll add an extra five. The rest of you, we're out of here in twenty four bound for Arizona; so get your acts together and grab some sunscreen, 'cause it's game on."

The disappointment was obvious. They were hoping for a few more days of chilling out. They hadn't even caused any serious trouble on base yet. At least one of them usually ended up in the guardhouse within the first forty eight hours. This was going to dent their reputation. But the road trip itself would take two to three days anyway, so not all was lost. Hilly was the most dejected out of the team but Jefferson knew that she'd be a bit more human after a good stretch of the legs.

Chapter 9
Stalemate

In the AMARS complex, tents had been deployed among which was an army canteen, so Hooper had a full stomach as well as a decent bit of sleep to his name. There were also a fair number of soldiers wandering about so he felt more at home. Smith had slept on one of the company's first aid beds overnight but Hooper had managed to convince him to get something a little more substantial than doughnuts in his body. So Smith had gone on the hunt for a hot meal. Where he would find one wasn't Hooper's problem.

A degree of confusion had been caused when the robot had requested more information from the mainframe. It had wanted to know the rules of driving on the roads. As it might contribute to safety they'd decided to let the robot have the necessary manuals for road etiquette. Although it didn't have indicators or brake lights, it did have arms so could use hand signals. They had tried to envisage how the robot would cope with that, but their imaginations weren't up to the task so they wrote it off as one of those things.

It had, however, prompted a heated discussion on whether they should contact driving schools in the area to warn them. After a good deal of consideration, the decision had been an emphatic, 'no.' It went that way after they spent a while arguing what, exactly, they would be telling people. Self driving cars weren't big news any more but a car that turned up at a driving school wanting to pass its own test, would send out completely the wrong message and see hoards of press involved in short order. Exactly what they didn't want right now.

The Signals soldier raised his head from the radio and announced, "Sir, there's been a possible sighting in Scottsdale."

Hooper groaned. "There's got to be upwards of fifty courses out there. Do we have any more information?"

"Yes Sir." The soldier passed him a piece of paper with co-ordinates on it.

Hooper got up and went to the map on the wall. He looked up the area and tapped it thoughtfully with his finger. "OK, deploy troops to all courses in this area," he said, drawing a circle with his finger, "and this time, side arms only and orders not to draw unless..." he faltered.

"Unless what, Sir?"

Hooper stood there for a while considering his next words carefully. "Unless fired upon. And even then if it's the robot doing the shooting well..."

"Well what, Sir?"

Hooper sighed. If he had been honest about it the order would have been something like, 'Run for your life.' but the most formal way he could translate his intention was, "Tactically retreat with all possible haste."

At that moment Smith walked in. He was a little bit calmer now that there wasn't so much sugar in his system. It was also a comfort that someone other than him was now ultimately responsible for taming the metallic beast; which was no doubt currently driving itself all over the highways amassing tickets for traffic violations. While Smith scanned the room for any new changes he saw Hooper's enthused behaviour and the purposeful look in his face. Smith immediately perked up. "News?"

"Yes. Possible sighting in this area." Hooper tapped the map. "I'm sending troops out to find it. Odds on it will hide in a golf course again."

The phone on Smith's desk rang. He picked it up. "Hello?"

"This is the main gate Sir. You wanted to know when the doughnut machine person came on site. She's just arrived."

"Thanks." Smith put the phone down, and wiped his face with his hands in an effort to pull himself together. After taking a few deep breaths he told Hooper that he'd be back in a few minutes, left operations again and took the familiar walk to the vending machines. He didn't quite believe what he was about to do but as one of their better customers he thought he deserved his say. By the time he rounded the corner a young woman was already there, filling up the trays. "Excuse me young lady. I wanted a word with you about this machine."

"Yes, sir; what can I do for you?"

"I'd like to put my vote in for more coffee flavoured ring please. There just aren't enough of them in here."

She picked up her clip board, extracted the pen and studied the paperwork. "I'm sorry sir, but there isn't enough room in this unit. All the choices are being bought and to give you more, we'd have to give someone else, less."

Smith was flabbergasted at this. "Well, what about that banana flavoured thing? Can't you remove that one?"

"Sorry sir. It's policy to always keep one slot open for new products."

"New products? What's wrong with the old ones? How many new toppings can you actually put on a doughnut for crying out loud?"

"Well, we've got experimental flavours coming out all the time. In fact I've got some samples of the latest on the van if you'd like to try one."

"Um, well, what is it?"

"It's a really innovative, bold invention that we're putting out there, that we're hoping will make big waves with the doughnut eating public."

Smith got the impression that she was trying to stall, as if she felt that there was something to hide about this new invention. "Yes, that's all fine, but what exactly is it?"

She went a little shy and shuffled her feet. "It's bacon flavour."

"Bacon flavour? Are you serious?"

She tried to pick up a mock enthusiasm for her work. "It isn't just bacon flavour sir. It's maple glazed bacon, crumbled, then sprinkled over a succulent glazed doughnut. Would you like to try one and give us your opinion?" she said hopefully, putting on a fake smile.

"I can give you my opinion right here without even needing to taste it. What the heck possessed you to even think about producing something like that?"

"Well, the doughnut market is very stagnant. The banana flavour was the newest thing that we've had for years and once that was done, well, we had to break new ground."

Smith sighed. He really had heard it all now. Bacon flavoured doughnuts. He was clearly up against a brick wall here. "Look. Is there any way you can run this by a superior please? I buy a lot of coffee flavour doughnuts from you and I'd just like a few more in the machine, that's all."

"I'll see what I can do sir. Anything else?"

"Er, no thanks." Smith turned and walked back to operations.

In the mean time groups of soldiers were in Scottsdale, descending on unsuspecting golf courses.

"Mulligan's Island," was a course built around a series of lakes. It was owned by Guy Clarkson, a repeat offender in the failed businessman stakes. He always managed to overlook a key factor in his dealings but somehow overcame his self-imposed lunacy and came out of one failed enterprise after another with just enough money to enable him to move on to the next disaster.

For instance, there was the time when he decided to go in to the marquee business. Thinking he had spotted a gap in the market he stocked up with lots of smaller units believing that they could be put together in arrangements that were more creative than the large ones. As it turned out, the amount of man hours required to assemble lots of small marquees quickly ate in to his profits and he had to abandon ship.

Fortunately, as the marquees were roughly car sized he managed to convince someone that they could sell them at events as portable garages and thus make a profit. After all, people who were displaying their beloved classic cars at open air shows would want to protect them from the elements, right? Some hapless soul signed on the dotted line and committed himself to buying Clarkson's entire stock. Due to the simple fact that he hadn't actually lied and the bloke had signed of his own free will, Guy won the inevitable court case. The money he eventually received, combined with the remainder of his savings and some fast talking at the bank, enabled him to buy Mulligan's Island.

He had taken a punt on making a golf course there because the land was relatively cheap. It was only after he had done all the work in building the place that he found out why the experienced club owners had stayed away from it. The amount of water turned the course in to a serious hazard for decent play and, after numerous golfers had complained about the number of, "mulligans," they had to take in the course of their game, he decided to make Mulligan's Island the name of the club and tried to make a feature out of how difficult it was to play on.

The only real challenge he faced now was the uphill battle in getting and retaining members.

Already weary from his years of tough business, the sight of two soldiers turning up at his humble venue, with rifles slung over their shoulders instead of golf clubs, set alarm bells ringing. There was trouble ahead, of that he was certain. When they fed him the now re-envisaged story of golf cart vandals operating in the area, he didn't actually buy into what they were selling him but he retained his composure. He was painfully aware that you don't call the military a bunch of liars and expect to get off without a fight, whether verbal or physical. As he wasn't in the mood for either flavour of disagreement he simply waved them in the direction of the cart shed and left them to it.

Sure enough they found the robot and immediately closed the club.

After waving and saying farewell to the last of his customers as they headed out the door, Guy quizzed the soldiers. "This isn't simple vandalism, is it?"

The soldiers looked at each other and wondered what they were going to tell the poor man. He had little enough business as it was and they'd effectively just scared away the last of his paying guests, severely damaging whatever little reputation that wasn't already in tatters. One of them broke and said, "Sir, it is perfectly true. It is a very serious and unusual issue of golf cart sabotage." Guy looked the soldier deep in the eyes and concluded that, yes, he was actually being told the truth. This had only been possible, of course, because the soldier conveniently left out the part that it was actually the "golf cart," that was doing all the damage. However, Guy concluded that this was as much information as he was going to get, and let the military have the run of the place. At the end of the day he couldn't stop them from descending on his little club anyway.

Maybe there would be a chance for compensation from all this. Yes. Compensation. That was something positive to think about. After all, he was a very regular customer of a particularly good law firm; they should be able to extract quite a healthy profit from this insanity.

There now existed a very awkward stalemate between the robot and the army. So long as the soldiers did nothing to spook the robot it had no reason to run. As long as the robot didn't run they at least had a handle on the situation. Translated, that meant that the soldiers had a handle on a situation that just happened to condescend to give them a convenient handle to hold on to in the first place. It was a handle of illusion; but it was at least something. Or nothing. Depending on how you looked at it.

Hooper and Smith settled in and waited for Jefferson and his team to arrive.

In the mean time the team itself was on the road. Duds was on his Suzuki Boulevard C90T. A comfortable tourer, he had a few extras fitted like the chrome oval mirrors, floorboard covers, Mustang seats and, a must for him, the extra jumbo, 'Saddlemen Desperado,' saddlebags, because he never knew what he was going to be asked to blow up next. One further modification that Duds had made to all his bikes was a button panel on the handlebars. The panel had a plastic cover and underneath it was a bank of six buttons that he could use to trigger explosive charges. He was wearing a three-quarter helmet, fitted with a radio so he could talk with the rest of the team in the RV, but still enjoy a bit of the fresh, rushing air.

Bunny was driving and the other three were sat around her discussing the mission. Jefferson had shared out bits of the robot specs.

"This is one bad ass piece of kit." ventured Hawkeye.

"And it's running a chess program?" queried Hilly. "How'd they get away with that?"

"The other supporting systems." said Bunny. She'd digested the whole folder already and, with her grounding in electronics and software, found it a refreshing change from the usual game of, 'track the enemy transmissions.' She continued. "The systems around the main core translate the world for the program."

Hilly filled in the blanks. "So it hasn't actually got a clue that it isn't playing on a chess board?"

"Exactly. It's just an algorithm that's interpreting what it's fed and then gives back general instructions."

Jefferson looked up from the folder. "Particularly deadly ones by the looks of it."

Over the radio link Duds joined in. "Does it have any weaknesses?"

Hawkeye piped up. "Not that I can see; they've done a good job of this all right. All the joints are covered and the armour might be able to stand a heavy round. We're going to have to get to the design team to find out more detail on it; there just isn't enough information in here."

Hilly piped up again. "So what's the plan boss?"

Jefferson took a deep breath. "Well, looking at

this, we aren't going to be able to kill this thing with our usual weapons. We're going to have to make a trap and lead it in."

Hilly leant back, folded her arms and huffed, "Great. Traps mean bait and I know what that usually means. And by the looks of this thing it doesn't take prisoners."

Jefferson tapped her on the shoulder. "Actually, it does." He held up the section of paperwork that detailed the wrist capture and cable tie function.

"Oh great. That's all we need."

Chapter 10
A Plan

The guard at the entrance to AMARS had been told who to expect. When she saw a dust cloud in the distance, she knew who and what was coming. Duds was riding in front of the RV so that he wouldn't have to contend with the sand that Bunny's beast kicked up. He was the first to reach the complex so pulled over to the guard hut, kicked the stand down, killed the engine and took his helmet off. By the time he'd done this he heard the RV pull up behind him and the air brakes engage.

Duds dismounted and unzipped his jacket "Morning Ma'am. We're here on the orders of General Hooper." He made a gesture to reach inside his jacket and raised his eyebrows in question. The guard nodded in return. Keeping his movements slow, he reached in to get his ID. Bringing it out at a respectful speed he presented it to the guard.

She took it and looked it over. "Sure. I was told to expect you." The others approached and handed over their ID cards as well. The guard inspected them all. "I was told not to bother asking to check your vehicles over, so carry on through and follow the sound of the drill sergeant's yelling. In the highly unlikely event that your engines drown out his lungs, then the signs to operations are what you need to follow." She handed back their ID's, waved them in the general direction of ops and retreated to her hut.

"Sounds like she isn't a fan of the military."

muttered Hilly.

Jefferson offered a counterpoint. "Judging by the amount of hardware that's just been parked on her lawn I can see why. OK people, let's go."

They mounted up and when they started to roll forward, the guard raised the barrier and they entered the base. It didn't take too long before they reached the entrance to operations where Bunny's RV promptly blocked in several cars. If they wanted out it was tough luck.

After presenting themselves to building security they signed the usual paperwork, got the visitor name tags for their uniforms, which they pinned underneath the name tags already sewn on, and were led up to where General Hooper had made his home.

Although the area was fairly large in itself, when any number of people came through the door to ops at the same time, they made an impact. Jefferson, complete with team, certainly did that. As they walked in Smith reflected that he was about to take a pounding in the game of, 'ops floor territory.'

Introductions didn't take too long and it was relatively easy to work out who needed to know what. Bunny went to the Hydra lab to learn more about the robots technology and logical weaknesses. Hawkeye and Duds went to the hanger to talk with Hicks about the physical aspects of the robot, while Hilly and Jefferson stayed with Hooper and Smith to talk tactics.

"OK Sir," Jefferson said to Hooper once they had all been split up and settled. "The way I see it is we've got two options. If we find a weakness then we take it out where it sits. Otherwise we're going to have to lure it in to a trap somehow."

Hooper agreed. "We were thinking pretty much the same thing. These folks know the robot and your team knows all about things that go bang, so between everyone here we should be able to come up with a plan." He turned to Smith. "Is there a conference room that we can take over? Somehow I don't think we're going to be able to fit everyone in here comfortably."

"Yes, down the corridor." said Smith relieved that he wasn't going to lose more of his precious floor space.

"Good. Let's get some of this paperwork down there while we wait for Jefferson's guys to do their talking."

Meanwhile, over at Mulligan's Island the soldiers were doing what all good soldiers do when there's nothing on the schedule; namely, take advantage of the situation.

A number of them had decided to use the opportunity to improve their handicap but were rapidly coming to the conclusion that this course wasn't doing them any favours. They used the excuse that it was good exercise because, for obvious reasons, they couldn't get access to any of the golf buggies and had to walk their clubs around the course. Not that they actually needed excuses. They were there for a number of days so boredom had to be relieved somehow and the new past time of shooting golf carts had been removed from the menu faster than it had been put on it in the first place.

Guy didn't mind too much. He was making more profit from the bar than he had made in memberships all year. He made a mental note that self-driving golf carts were apparently good for business.

Some of the soldiers weren't too happy with their easy guard duty, however. They were discussing what they would say to their children when they returned from the assignment. It would be a case of telling their offspring that they had been urgently sent on top secret government business, supported by a touch of their nose, a secretive wink and a hope that the kids left it at that. Somehow it was considered a more honourable thing to do than openly admit that they had spent the week guarding a golf course.

Back at AMARS it had taken a day and a half before the team was satisfied they had gone through all the angles. Everyone was sat around the large circular table. Smith was off to one side as was Hicks. This was Hoopers show now.

"OK, so options for destroying this thing where it stands."

Jefferson leant forward. "No go. The amount of force needed would be too great where it is and it has extra ordnance on board. We need to get it away from there at the very least before we bombed it. Also if we started erecting shielding around it, then there's a chance it would work out what we were doing and take off again anyway."

"Are there any weak points in it?"

Hawkeye leant forward. "Yes, the armour gets a little thinner on the back of the neck stalk but to get at it, the thing has to be unpacked in its erect form. Even then there's no guarantee that any particular shot in the wild will do it. Testing on the range had mixed results depending on the angle of the bullet when it hit. It's got a tough, multi layered skin."

Hooper sat back. "Ok, so if we set this thing running can we track it?"

Bunny had this one covered. "No. It's heavily shielded and it gives out very little heat. Only when it talks with the mainframe does it put out signals and even then it could be on any of a range of frequencies. If we deliberately wanted to track it we'd need to give it a sugar coated frequency and then we could triangulate its position; but that will obviously only work within a limited area and even then, only as long as it's talking. Eyes hot is the only sure way to do this."

Hooper considered all the information. "So." He tapped his fingers on the desk. "We need to set up a powerful trap, somewhere where it can't see us do it and then lure it in. Also, we need to get it to ditch some of its ammunition on the way if we can. That sound about right?" The team looked at each other and nodded.

Hooper turned around to look at the map. "There's plenty of abandoned towns in New Mexico. If we teased it out there we could do the job."

Bunny scuppered that idea. "The buildings out there aren't substantial enough. Its sensors would easily pick up any odd walls that were thicker than they should be, along with any live wiring in a town that's supposed to be empty. Too risky. Wherever we do this, it needs to be somewhere busy. Buildings, electrical signals, a live town with so much going on that the robot will have a lot to analyse and hopefully overlook anything slightly odd."

That news didn't go down too well. Silence hung over the meeting room as Hooper considered the options, turning over the limited choices in his mind. Eventually, he got up, walked to the map, tapped on an area in New Mexico and stated simply, "Roswell." Then he started tracing his finger all the way back to Phoenix. "It will also give the robot a decent run to get there and we can use that journey to tease it in to firing what its got at us. The population in Roswell will be used to strange things being talked about. Heck, even if word does get out the only people that will actually believe news reports of a robot running wild, are the ones already wearing tin foil head gear. I think we can safely pull this off without causing too much of a fuss." He turned to Smith. "I'm going to need your help in getting that damn robot to go where we need it to go though."

Smith sighed, "Roswell sounds like a good option. Hell, actual UFOs could land there and no one would think anything of it." Hooper shot him a suspicious glance as if to say, 'Who told you about that?' but re-ran Smith's words in his head and concluded that it was only an off-the-cuff comment. Smith probably didn't actually know anything so he returned to the task at hand.

Hooper picked up a marker and drew a line between Mulligan's Island and Roswell. "OK, the robots route would be difficult both in terms of the terrain and the political fall out. It takes in the San Carlos reservation, Gila National Forest and the Mescalero reservation. That little lot is going to be a nightmare."

Smith stepped forward and offered a ray of hope. "Actually," he said, making sweeping motions to the south, "the robot will want the method of least resistance." He was highlighting the road network. "All that wooded and mountain terrain wouldn't help it get anywhere very quickly. The moment it thinks it needs maps for anything outside Arizona, it will ask the mainframe. With a bit of programming and massaging some figures we can very likely convince it to go south and avoid the reservations and mountains." He drew a line down from the golf course to Cactus Falls and then over towards Denning. "The interstate would give it a real speed advantage." He continued drawing east. "Then when it hits Las Cruces, there's the seventy which takes it through the mountain range," he swept up with the board marker, "through the Mescalero reservation and in to Roswell. If it swallows the bait we'll even have the advantage of knowing how it intends to approach."

Hooper drew himself up and addressed the room. "OK people. It looks like we're about to leave gaping holes all over interstate ten, scare the crap out of some small towns, cause a diplomatic incident with a Native Indian tribe and create minor chaos in a population of fifty thousand people. Before we pull the trigger on this insanity does anyone have *any* other ideas?"

He surveyed the room but was met only with

silence.

Finally, Hooper sucked up his chest. "Right. Lets make this happen, people. Smith, you're going to make sure that when we lay the bait the robot goes the way we want it to go. I'm going to get some traps laid along the way that will make it use its heavy ammo." He pointed at Jefferson. "I need a plan for what happens when the robot gets there." He finished by addressing Bunny. "Adams, talk with your new programming buddies and see what might make that robot haul ass."

"Yes, Sir." she saluted. The meeting broke up and everyone went about their tasks, except Hooper who sat back and wondered how he was going to explain to the tribal chairman of the Mescalero that they were about to stampede a rampant, heavily armed robot through the reservation. He sighed. The things he had to do in his job were sometimes completely off the wall and there were days when he just wished he was a private again.

Twenty four hours later they were all back at the table. Hooper led again. "Right. Lets take this from the top. Smith, have you done the programming?"

"Yes. The team have laid in all the figures. There's still no guarantee that the robot will take it. It might do its own research and upset the Navaho and Sioux anyway; but we'll cross that bridge if it decides to cross their reservations."

Hooper picked up again and gestured at the map. "I've arranged some expendable drones to attack it from the air. The moment it leaves Phoenix and gets into safe territory," he ran his hand around the south east of Phoenix, "we attack it and hopefully cause it to use its surface to air missiles. That'll be a chunk of the ordnance out the way." Hooper then swept his arm to the east of Cactus Flat. "Remote control tanks will attack it in this area and with luck it will use its rockets against them. That should leave it with just the more conventional weapons and it will be relatively safe to explode when we get to Roswell. Over to you." he finished, pointing at Jefferson.

Jefferson rose from his seat with a large sheet of paper. Pinning it over the top of the general map, it showed a close up of Roswell's centre. "The plan is to bring it to Roswell and tease it to this location." He tapped a point on the map. "To the west we have Wells Fargo Bank on, 'North Pennsylvania.' Nice tall building that Duds can use to eyeball the robot coming in and oversee everything from there. To the east we have the court house. In between them are these two buildings on, 'Richardson Avenue,' with a narrow alley between them and a car park behind. Duds is going to line the walls with shaped charges and when we lure the thing in there, then it's hopefully, 'goodnight robot.'" He swept his arm slightly further up North Pennsylvania. "A little up here is a church with a bell tower. With Hawkeye up there he should be able to see over the post office building. He can loose off an armour piercing round at the back of the robots neck if it doesn't take the bait."

Hooper liked what he saw but he took a closer look at the markings on the map. "Those two buildings. Is that one actually Roswell's public safety office?"

Jefferson hesitated a bit. "Yes, Sir. It is. Totally unintentional irony there I assure you. It just happened to have a suitable alley."

Hooper settled back in to his chair. "Well, I guess we don't have that much choice. Only one thing left to tidy up now. Exactly what *is* the bait?"

"Me." said Jefferson. "I'm hoping that if we program fake information to the robot that I've got a new weapon that can kill it, that I'm located in that car park behind the building and that my intention is to come for it, then it might come for me first. With some carefully placed barricades we should be able to corral it in to going exactly where we want it."

This all seemed to be the kind of, 'seat of the pants,' stuff that Hooper didn't like so much. "Can we do this?" he turned to Smith for confirmation.

"Yes, the team can invent a fictional Hydra killing weapon. There's a lot of theory about portable rail guns, high powered lasers and the like that we don't yet know how to put in to practice but the robot won't know that. I'm fairly sure we can convince it that it's in real danger."

It was all very high risk. "And what are the odds that it will actually take this bait and come out from its hidey hole?" Hooper continued.

Bunny leant forward, "Actually, roughly fifty fifty according to the programming teams. If we keep broadcasting the same information at infrequent intervals along with the mundane updates, then each time we do it we force the robot to toss the coin, logically speaking."

Hooper completed the theory. "So no matter

how often it runs the odds, it's only got to land on heads once."

"Exactly Sir."

He was convinced. "OK, Jefferson. Mount up for Roswell. I'll talk with the mayor there and get everything straightened out. Hopefully we'll get all this done with minimal damage." He had other calls to make as well, such as declaring a no-fly zone to keep the press helicopters out and a general reporting blackout on anything that was about to happen in Roswell.

Chapter 11
Minimal Damage

The team had taken up position in Roswell. The RV had been parked in an area to the east; opposite from where the robot would approach. Hilly and Jefferson were in town giving Duds a hand laying the charges.

Earlier that day, people had been asked to vacate the town centre and most had heeded the warning. The staff of the two buildings they were going to use, however, were asked to help empty their offices. Not only didn't they like having to move out at short notice but, when they overheard Duds saying that they were getting the latest in modern air conditioning, in the form of great big holes in the brickwork, they started to kick up a fuss. Actually, the damage caused by the explosives would likely mean that both buildings would have to be demolished and re-built, a fact that Duds decided to keep to himself rather than create wholescale panic.

It took intervention by someone high up in Town Hall and promises of this, that and the other before some very upset and reluctant people resigned themselves to a temporary relocation from their comfortable offices. Soldiers were brought in to help get things packed and shifted as quickly as possible. Time was of the essence and they were out of options.

As they worked on the charges, Hilly caught sight of a small book resting on Dud's tool wrap. It was blackened and had scorch marks on it. "What's this? 'Journal of H.R.Dudman.' Your dad?"

Duds stopped in the middle of stripping some wires, turned to Hilly, took a screwdriver out of his mouth and replied. "Yup. That was my Dad's journal. He was in demolition and bomb disposal. Took that journal everywhere. He wrote down all the jobs he did so he could reference them again."

Hilly flipped through the book. "Wow. Interesting stuff."

Duds returned to his work. "I've learned a hell of a lot from those pages over the years."

After spending a few moments reading some of the pages, Hilly's attitude changed a little. She got a little sad and put down the book. "Well, I'm going to get a breath of air. Back in a bit."

"Cool." said Duds absent mindedly as he continued with the wire stripping.

Jefferson noticed the change in Hilly. "You know, Duds, I think I'll join her. Could do with a bit of a break." He followed her out. She was leaning up against a wall looking sad. He walked over to her. "Hey, what's up?"

"Oh, just the journal that's all."

"Dud's father? What was wrong with it?"

"The last page."

Jefferson suddenly understood what she was talking about. "What did it say?"

"Well, he was working on a home made terrorist time bomb. The notes briefly outlined the set up and it was ticking down with no way to know how long was left on the clock. The last words written were, 'Going for the blue wire.'"

"Oh." Jefferson leant against the wall and joined Hilly in a few minutes of quiet reflection. He wondered whether this was the reason why Duds showed so little fear in his work.

In the mean time the word was passed around the neighbouring businesses that there was an emergency that had to be dealt with, and that there were going to be controlled explosions, resulting in imploding glass and all that came with it. The few who had decided to ignore the initial instruction to vacate, then suddenly remembered that they'd left their lunch at home or had to pick up the kids early from school. Miraculously, very few people were curious enough to ask what the emergency actually was. 'Dealing with dangerous munitions,' was all that the soldiers told them. After all it wasn't too far from the truth.

It was a fair few hours of drilling, cabling and testing before Duds was finally happy that his shaped charge, 'brick sandwich,' was nicely buttered and ready for its robot filling. Tired and uncertain of what lay ahead, they headed back to the RV and a very restless sleep.

The following day, everything was in place. "OK," said Smith. "All set here. Ready to proceed on your order General."

Hooper held his breath. It was all on his command now and these sorts of decisions never rested lightly on his shoulders, even when an operation had been planned as meticulously as this. He pondered how his career had got to this point. All he had done with his life was follow his father in to the military as he had followed his father before him. Strict upbringing, pride in the flag, strong sense of right and wrong, all that had been instilled in him long before he signed the enlistment papers.

He started his career in the infantry and worked his way up, achieving his first star in his forties. Now here he was, recently turned fifty, nursing a bunch of technology companies who were making more trouble for him in peace time than he ever had to cope with during war. Was this the reward for giving his best years to the service? A desk job and a pension? On the one hand it seemed right, but on the other he still yearned to be at the front line even though, deep down, he knew that he'd likely break a hip if he ever went on pack drill again. It was his experience that was more valuable than his strength now.

That knowledge had limits, however. In theatre, things were more or less scripted. Lessons had been learned over hundreds of years. There were historical battles with detailed accounts of the fighting. From those, leaders had forged plans of action which, themselves, added to the military lore which was passed down through the generations. He was pretty sure that there was nothing in the entire archive of military history, however, that could have prepared him to deal with an intelligent golf cart, equipped with a sniper rifle that could shoot smoke from its rear end and tear gas from its…

"General?" prompted Smith. "We're waiting for your order."

Hooper snapped back to the present. "Let loose the dogs of war. Let's go." He turned to the Signals soldier. "Launch the drones and let me know when they're in a holding pattern over Mulligan's Island."

"Yes Sir."

If the tension in the air had mass, then they wouldn't have been able to see their hands in front of their faces. Nerves were on high alert and Smith already had a stash of coffee flavour doughnuts by his keyboard. This was going to be a long one. The second hand on the wall clock achieved a density previously known only in specialist research communities and each tick could have been measured on the Richter scale.

Finally, the feedback came. "Drones in position Sir."

"Ok, Smith, down to you."

Smith addressed the operative overseeing the mainframe. "Broadcast the information about Jefferson and the made-up weapon to the robot."

"Yes, Sir."

They waited with bated breath for news from the golf course. The soldiers on the ground had already been told not to stand in the way of the robot and under no circumstances to challenge it or get in its way, but there was always the chance that someone would panic and let a round off.

What would the robot do next? Smith's nerves were on edge and Hooper rose from his chair as they watched the monitors in front of them. As well as the attack drones sent in to tease the missiles out of the Hydra, there were three others on tracking duty watching everything and ready to follow the robot wherever it went. There was no telling whether this thing would move or not and, if it did, in which direction it would go. The only thing they could be sure of was that if it did move, it would be damn quick.

Silence hung like lead in the operations room.

"Sir!" came a shout from the mainframe operative. "It's swallowed the map for New Mexico and also the directions."

Hooper stepped towards Smith. "For a powerful machine it's sure taking its damn time making its mind up."

Smith, not taking his eyes off the screens, turned his head slightly towards Hooper. "It's got a lot of scenarios to run and this is a touch more complicated than moving plastic pieces around a chequered board."

Hooper followed Smith's eyes to the screen and the pair of them stood there watching the live feeds from the golf course and the drones. So far nothing had moved from the shed. Over the airwaves a sniper with a vantage point, reported. "It's still in there. No movement seen."

Suddenly it made a break for it and the sniper updated their report. "Fuck! That thing can move. Um, sorry Sir; target has left the building and is mobile." The robot had shot out of the shed and was fast making its way east.

"It's taken the bait." Smith said, reaching for a doughnut.

The drone feeds showed the Hydra turn south, trying to steer clear of the general population. Obviously it couldn't avoid the large number of golf courses and there were countless golfers who suffered detriments to their score sheets that day.

Balls were sliced, concentration shattered and drive shots ended up woefully underpowered as golfers were distracted by an unmanned, battleship grey golf cart hurtling its way across greens, over fairways and occasionally catching air as it hit the humps and bumps that formed the tee-off points.

Eventually it made contact with the tarmac of the seventy nine and hurtled through Florence. Its head section was slightly extended so that it could analyse the traffic ahead. It was able to time its movements to jump the lights and not hit anything, but behind it chaos ensued as cars collided, horns sounded and irate people shouted and gestured, both at each other and the speeding robot. Smith and Hooper watched all this from the control centre. At the same time, many miles away in an RV parked in a field to the east of Roswell, Jefferson and his team were viewing that same feed with amazement. "Damn it." commented Hilly. "That thing can really move."

When the robot was clear of the populated area it went off road in an obvious attempt to switch to Interstate Ten. "Now," commanded Hooper. "Attack with the drones." Signals conveyed the order and the initial wave of battle commenced.

The first drone came in from behind the robot, targeted it and launched its, 'radar killer,' air-to-ground missile. The robot sensed the lock and raised one of its own surface to air missiles which it launched at the drone. They wanted the robot to think its missiles would do the job so they were prepared to let the drone get blown out of the sky. What they weren't prepared for, however, was how the Hydra would react to the missile that they were throwing at it.

The robot turned on the spot and started running as fast in reverse as it was going forward. It unpacked its sniper rifle just enough to be able to use it, took aim and shot the incoming missile right out of the sky. It was all combined into a super fast, smooth ballet of action. "Did that thing just..." Hawkeye stuttered as he watched the monitor.

"Yup." said Bunny, unable to believe what she had just seen. She knew that electric motors could act fast but to see them work this quick was unbelievable.

With the exchange complete, the robot took a few moments to gather itself. The sniper rifle and missile launcher that it had opened in the heat of battle, took a few seconds to be packed away again. Once it was all nice and streamlined, it turned its forward sensors back to the direction of travel and resumed its breakneck journey to the interstate.

"What the hell have you got us into boss?" Duds questioned. Jefferson could find no words to respond and Hilly decided to stop watching and exited the RV, grabbing a bottle of iced tea from the fridge on her way out. Jefferson felt he should have made her watch so that she knew what they were up against, but he thought that maybe she had already seen enough.

Back in the operations centre Hooper put his hands on Smith's shoulder. "You know, if that robot wasn't completely screwed up I'd want a dozen of those things on my side." He turned to the Signals soldier. "Let the second drone loose. I want the other missile out of that robot before it hits the interstate."

"Yes Sir."

The order was given and the same events unfolded. The drone launched its missile at the robot and the robot returned fire. The drone exploded in flames while the robot shot the missile out of the air, just like it was a paper aeroplane. Hooper dispatched teams to clear up the mess and pondered on the cost equation of radar-killers verses sniper rounds.

With the first job done, the next was to ensure that all the remote control tanks converged on the interstate further east. It was something like four hundred miles between Phoenix and Les Cruces and Hooper had picked a spot roughly half way between Tucson and Dening to ambush the robot with the tanks. They had initially been well spaced out in case the Hydra went north but as they continued to track it, the tanks started to trundle to the expected ambush point. As the robot left San Simon the tanks would be waiting to take it on.

The next couple of hours were nail biting in the RV. Discussion was heated as they saw their greatest adversary yet, chewing up the miles between Phoenix and them. Here was a formidable opponent that didn't have human flaws. It wouldn't pin you down in a hopeless position and then start monologuing its plans for global domination at you. It would just fire. There would be no second chances just instant, precision action and that rightfully scared the crap out of them.

Hawkeye was still running the choice of

Windrunner .50 or CheyTac .408 through his mind. He went outside stopping for a moment to exchange sombre glances with Hilly, before going round to the other side of the RV where he had a reinforced store similar to Duds'.

Pulling one of his drawers out he fingered two of his most favoured weapons. His chest felt heavy and tense. In his soul he knew that there would only be a need for a single round. If he screwed up there would be no opportunity for a second shot.

Drawing a breath between his clenched teeth he picked up the .50 and slung it over his shoulder. He put the drawer back in and pulled out another from which he selected a small box of armour piercing rounds and a pair of binoculars for good measure. He then pushed the drawer closed and secured the storage unit before walking back around to the door and standing beside Hilly; neither of them saying a word.

Inside, the team were watching the fight. The light tanks were having a hard time with the robot. The battle was raging at the border of Arizona and New Mexico. The tanks couldn't target the robot effectively because it was just too fast. The only chance they had was when it slowed down for long enough to unpack itself, eject its rocket pack and let loose a deadly kiss goodnight to one of their metal brethren. It was inevitable that the robot would breach the defences and when it was finally on its way again, Hooper looked at Smith in operations. "Two." Smith said. "It's still got two rockets on board."

"That's not good." replied Hooper, who started

pacing a little. "Can we get any more out?"

"Not unless you've got any more tanks between there and Roswell."

"No. We haven't. The ones that survived aren't fast enough to chase that thing down." He keyed the mike. "Jefferson, the robot still has two rockets on board."

"OK Sir," crackled the response.

Back in the RV Jefferson turned to the team, "It's game on. Positions people."

Bunny moved her chair slightly so that she was directly in front of her consoles. To her right sat the pink rabbit. She worried its ear as she always did when she got nervous. Various listening stations had been placed around Roswell along with a single military repeater. The idea was that the robot would be coaxed into using the repeater, allowing Bunny to use the listening stations to triangulate the robot whenever it talked back to the mainframe.

Duds mounted up his Suzuki and Hilly got on behind him. They remained silent as Duds kicked the engine in to action and they rode off in to town.

From the back of the RV Jefferson unhooked Duds' motocross bike. He and Hawkeye mounted up and followed Duds and Hilly into battle.

It wasn't long before they were in position. Duds was on top of the Wells Fargo building with the ability to see the robot when it approached from the west, as well as see the eventual action between the target buildings. Hawkeye was positioned in the bell tower of the church. Hilly was in a light truck parked on Fifth with the engine running and Jefferson was in the car park where he had planned an escape route if everything went pear shaped.

Their hearts were in their mouths as they waited.

"What do we do if this goes tits up boss?" Hawkeye asked over the radio.

"We do what we always do. Improvise." That was the best Jefferson could offer him. "How we doing Bunny?"

"The drones were low on juice so they pulled away. We've got no eyeball on it until new drones arrive. Duds is our eyes now."

"Hear that Duds?" Jefferson repeated.

"Yeah I heard. No sign of it yet."

Waiting like this was more agonising than fighting. It was now afternoon; the majority of the day being spent on the other battles. There wasn't that much light left but more than enough for the short burst of hell that they were about to engage in.

Up in the bell tower Hawkeye was getting nervous. Most of the buildings were single storey so he could shoot over them but this was far from ideal. It was the best he was going to get though. The angle was precarious, sure, but he knew that wherever he took up station there was no guarantee which way the robot would be facing. To add to the pressure, if he shot before the robot moved in to the alley then he might cause it to change its path.

He knew that if the robot attempted to shoot Jefferson without actually moving in to the alley then the game would be up and the robot might get spooked anyway. If that happened he was the last chance. To shoot, or not to shoot. He didn't have any clear criteria on which to call it. No solid signal on whether to pull the trigger, or let it ride.

"Eyeball. Coming in fast." Duds exclaimed over the radio. "Route as planned."

The Hydra came in through West Second. A carefully parked bus helped to stop it from going on to Main unless it wanted some trouble so it turned up North Richardson as they hoped. When it hit the two buildings it turned to face the alley between them and instantly saw the image of Jefferson at the other end of it. Smaller than expected but it was unmistakably its target. Instead of going down the alley, however, the robot unpacked itself to standing position and started to raise its sniper rifle. At the same time it activated its extended sensor bank. If a mouse broke wind two streets away it would know about it. The laser sight locked on to Jefferson's head.

BANG went the Windrunner as Hawkeye loosed his round at the robot. The moment that he had seen it unpacking its rifle he concluded that it wasn't going to move into the trap, so he fired. It was the best shot he was ever going to get. After the round was away he didn't even stop to eject the cartridge. He used the action of the recoil to help him spin his body around, shoulder the gun and jump for the bell rope. He sent himself down through the hatch in a single, well practised, fluid move.

The robot knew the precise location of Hawkeye the moment he pulled the trigger so it simply turned to face the church, opened its rocket rack and fired. His round had been at such an angle that although it messed up the metal work in the robots neck, it hadn't gone in to any serious electronics. The robot was still fully functional.

By the time the rocket made contact with the tower, Hawkeye's head was already well below the hatch. As he was sliding down the rope there was a massive explosion above him as the top of the tower turned into a violent mess of flying brickwork. The shock wave forced him off to one side where he landed on one of the staging platforms. He groaned in pain from the hard landing as all around him, wood, stone and other pieces of the disintegrating tower fell to the floor below, leaving him stranded half way up the heavily damaged structure, choking in fresh dust.

A quick look down, told him that he wasn't getting out of this any time soon and a massive, "clang," from outside explained where the bell had landed. His earpiece was still intact. "I'm stuck here for a while, boss."

"Fine. No problem. Just stay quiet."

The robot opened its front door and sent its drone on a reconnaissance mission. It then closed its rocket bay and turned to face Jefferson once more. Quickly acquiring its target it let lose a sniper round which smashed the mirror at the end of the alley. Confused by this for a few moments the robot cautiously rolled in to the alley to determine what had become of its target.

It passed straight by the explosives and nothing happened. "Duds?" called Jefferson over the radio. "DUDS! What the hell's happening?" There was no response from the top of Wells Fargo. "Bunny?"

"No eyes here. Duds was all I had. Still no

drones yet and no radio chat happening either. I'm blind boss."

As the robot emerged into the car park on the other side of the buildings, it looked to either side and caught sight of Jefferson stood between two parked trucks. It saw him as he turned and started running for his life. After its previous failure it upped its odds of taking the target down. It launched its capture net at the fleeing figure of Jefferson while simultaneously firing another sniper round at him. Again, there was a shattering of glass. A second mirror. Jefferson had used two mirrors to project his image to the attacking Hydra.

As the robot moved forward, delayed a little by having to force the trucks apart, Jefferson had hopped over a barrier and vanished behind a dumpster. When the robot reached the place where the mirror had been and started analysing the situation, the roar of the motocross engine filled the air. The robot moved to the barrier and ripped it out of the ground with ease. By the time it had barged the dumpster to one side and trundled onto the small patch of grass behind it, Jefferson was already making his way up North Main, swerving and ducking as he rode.

Before the robot had even managed to turn its body and begin to track him, Hilly drove the truck out of East Fifth and stopped it on the junction, preventing the Hydra from getting a straight line of sight. She then dropped out of the truck and raced towards the church where Hawkeye had been. The robot analysed Hilly but saw no weapons so didn't register her as a threat. It simply manoeuvred its way around the truck and gave chase to Jefferson who, by now, had turned off Main and was weaving a pattern through town, in the hope of being as difficult a target as possible. The robot's damaged neck was preventing it from closing down into chase mode, not that this hampered it a great deal. It started following Jefferson and that was the last the team saw of it as Hilly continued running towards the ruined church.

"Stay still Hawkeye." she radioed. "That drone thing is crossing the road. I think it's coming to make sure it's finished the job." In the RV, Bunny heard this and broke the link between the short wave frequencies of the team radio and the longer ones that Hooper was using. The last thing they needed was Hooper's demands for an update in their ears while they were fighting for their lives. She could relay anything important.

Hilly followed the small drone at a distance. She saw it making its way slowly up the steps with an arm extended. On the end of the arm were some sensors and what she recognised instantly as a gun barrel.

Hawkeye was shivering slightly. There was a deal of pain coming from his right hip but if he made a sound then the drone would know he was still alive. The only blessing was that it couldn't get up there. He closed his eyes and winced at the pain. As the adrenaline started to ease its way out of him, the pain became worse. 'Screw that damn round. The angle was too great. I shouldn't have taken the bloody shot. It was stupid, stupid, stupid.' he chided himself.

Below him, in the now pin-drop silence, he heard the electric motors of the drone as it entered the building. It slowly made its way through the centre of the aisles towards the front of the church where the debris had fallen and a grey dust was still hanging in the air. Hilly cautiously walked in behind it and feinted to one side. She saw the drone come to rest on top of the rubble and extend its sensors as much as it could up the gaping hole that used to be the bell tower.

Hilly didn't know what to do. She felt like jumping on top of it and wringing its scrawny little metallic neck, but she had no weapons. The best she could have done was to pick up a piece of broken wood and have at it; but that wouldn't end well. She had to keep her fear and anger inside her and wait to see what the bastard thing did.

For his part Hawkeye dare not even whisper. All had gone silent below him but he knew that it was just waiting for him to give it a shred of confirmation that he was still alive. Being a robot it could wait an awful long time for that and the pain in his hip was rising. Boom, boom, boom went his pulse in his ears. He hadn't seen this coming. His thoughts turned to Duds. What the hell had happened? He scrunched up his eyes and clenched his teeth with the pain.

Hilly was transfixed by the motionless robot. She almost daren't even breathe while she watched it just stand there, looking up what was left of the bell tower. What the hell would it do? With a human being you had some chance at being able to second guess them. You could get a clue as to what they were thinking by looking into their eyes, but a robot? Not a hope in hell.

She nearly jumped out of her skin when the drone finally moved. It retracted its sensors and reversed off the pile of rubble. It looked straight at her when it turned around but it left her alone and trundled out of the building, apparently satisfied that Hawkeye was dead. "It's leaving." she whispered on the radio after it was clear of the doors. "Give it a moment to get the hell out of here and then I can get you down." She jogged cautiously out of the church and saw it head north. Only once she was convinced that it was going to keep moving did Hilly look around for options. The vibrations caused by the rocket explosion had loosened some of the pews so she put her shoulder in to finishing the job and managed to get one of them free from the floor. Dragging it over to the bell tower she heaved it almost vertical, leant it at an angle against the wall and slowly climbed up to just below the platform where Hawkeye was laying. "You all right?"

"No. Hip. Agony." The pain was obviously affecting him.

"Can you get down here?"

"What option?" he said through clenched teeth.

"Well, none really."

Hawkeye's shaking arm handed her what was left of the Windrunner and she shouldered it before helping him slide himself to the edge of the platform. She took as much of his weight as she could and then gently allowed them both to slide down the pew. When they reached the bottom

Hawkeye yelped in pain.

"There's more of that to come, fella." Hilly stated.

"No joke. Why?"

"Gotta get in to Wells Fargo and find Duds."

"Arrgghhh..." was all that Hawkeye could manage as Hilly put his arm over her shoulder and helped him hobble across the street and into the modern glass building, watching carefully in case the robot or its little drone showed up again.

In the RV, Bunny was talking with Hooper. "We got our arse handed to us Sir. Duds went silent and the explosives didn't fire."

"Do we know why?"

"No Sir, we're trying to ascertain that now."

"Give me a report when you know. It's getting dark out there and the surveillance drones can't locate the robot. We don't know where it is."

"Neither do we, Sir. It's radio silent and not talking to the mainframe."

Meanwhile, Jefferson had made it all the way out to a waste treatment plant on the north east corner of town before he had even dared to look back over his shoulder. The robot seemed to have given up the chase. He had heard Hilly say that the Hydra had launched its little robot and there was a chance that, once deployed, it couldn't move too far away from the drone. He couldn't be sure, but that would be the most obvious reason as to why it stopped following him. "Bunny. Heard anything more?"

"No boss, still blind. Drones are overhead but can't find it. You OK?"

"Yes I'm fine. Shaken up. It gave me up for some reason. I think the drone tethered it."

"Very possibly. I'll ask AMARS."

Back in the Wells Fargo building Hilly had got Hawkeye in to a lift. He wanted to stay on the ground floor but Hilly reckoned that height was their safest option right now, so up they were going. He didn't quite know what was worse, the agony in his hip or the assault of the cheesy elevator music on his ears.

They were the only people in the building. The sudden arrival of the military and the considerable about of fuss that had been made, apparently had an impact. A good portion of the population suddenly remembered relatives in other parts of the country they hadn't seen for a while, and perhaps it was about time they paid them a visit. When Hilly and Hawkeye emerged from the lift into an eerily quiet reception area, Hawkeye made himself as comfortable as possible on a nearby sofa while Hilly went up to the roof.

She emerged in the fresh evening air to see Duds, unconscious in a small pile of rubble. A quick check showed it to be from the church. "It looks like some brickwork from the explosion made it up here, and knocked out Duds," she announced on the radio as she bent down to check his pulse. "He looks fine, just sleeping. Best make sure he gets a head scan when we're through this though."

"OK, keep me up to speed. I'll call it in now." replied Bunny.

Hilly turned the middle aged biker over on his back, took a small torch out from one of her trouser pockets and checked him over. He seemed clear. No fluid from the ears and also, no radio. It must have flown out somewhere. He'd be fine after a rest. As she put away her torch, Duds started to groan and come around. "Urgh. Did we get it?"

"No. It got you." she said, opening his eyelids further and looking for signs of concussion.

He winced. "Uh?"

"Brickwork from the church explosion landed on your skull. You could say it was a message from up above, from down below." Satisfied that he had escaped serious harm, she stood back and gave him some room.

"Oh hell." Duds reached for his head.

"Don't get up fast big fella. You've been out for a while."

"How long?"

"Don't really know. All this happened so fast. Ten minutes, fifteen tops."

"What's the status?"

"The status is that you don't even think about the status until you're all the way around." A quick glance found his radio not too far away, so while Duds nursed his aching head, Hilly retrieved it and gave it a clean up. "Here."

"Thanks."

"OK Boss," said Hilly, "We're all on the radio again."

"Good," Jefferson responded. "Well, we got pasted today and our target is somewhere unknown, presumably searching for me, back in hiding or some combination of the two so I'm staying away from the RV for now. You guys get back and dress your wounds. We're going to have to re-think this whole thing."

"Where are you going boss?" queried Bunny.

"I haven't got a clue yet and even if I did, I'm not going to announce it on-channel encrypted or not. We'll talk more when you get back to the RV." Jefferson gave the motocross a once over for any tracking devices and, satisfied that Hilly's truck diversion had worked, he settled down for an uneasy night certain in the knowledge that the Hydra didn't sleep.

Hilly eventually got Duds and Hawkeye out of the building and retrieved the truck. She loaded Duds' bike on to it and, with them in the back, made a bee line south until she was happy that the robot wasn't following them. That done she headed east and made her way to the RV.

When everyone was settled and the darkness was truly upon them, Bunny joined their personal radios with the wider band to Arizona and they all had a recap on what had happened. Bunny took her rabbit off the panel and sat with it on her lap. She turned to face the others, tugging at the rabbits ears.

"So what now?" asked Hilly in a bit of a huff.

Smith put something forward. "Well, the robot doesn't know about the charges so if we can get it to go through the gap again then maybe we stand a chance."

"And how, exactly, do you expect us to do that?" Hilly was still seriously pissed off with the way things had gone. "It's already been ambushed at that location. What kind of chances do your algorithm wonks give that the robot will repeat the same scenario?"

Silence was the reply from Arizona.

Bunny put something forward. "The only way we can form a plan is to know where the hell the robot is. The drone was seen moving north and that's all we know for sure. Has anyone got any ideas at all?"

Smith piped up over the radio again. "Well there is an army golf course to the north of there. If Jefferson is correct that it's gone back in to hiding then there is a good chance that it's picked another golf course."

"I'm pretty sure I did open up a gap on the back of its neck, though." offered Hawkeye. "That's got to be worth something, surely?"

Hilly was still in a foul mood. "What do you want us to do? Tell it that it looks a bit dirty, offer it a free car wash and hope it shorts itself?"

Jefferson piped up over the airwaves. "Knock it off, Hilly. I know it's been a rough day but we need some positive thinking here."

Hilly looked at her feet. "Sorry boss."

Jefferson took control. "Hilly, tomorrow morning I want you and Duds out at that golf course, unarmed, to try and find the thing. See if you can work out how much damage Hawkeye did."

"Yes boss."

"Bunny, call City Hall and get access to the local surveillance network. I want to know if you can use it to find out where the robot is, but also ask their network team if there's any hint of the robot using the same network to try and find me. If you've got the energy, then get started on that now."

"Yes boss." confirmed Bunny.

"Hawkeye..."

"Yes, boss."

"If you made a hole once I dare say you can get an incendiary round in to the same hole. Give it some thought."

"OK, boss."

"Anyone else got any ideas?" There was a reluctant chorus of silence both from Arizona and the RV. "OK, then lets get some sleep. I'll check in at 08:00. Need to save radio power. Night night."

Arizona signed off and left the team to it. Bunny picked up a mobile and called City Hall while the rest of them sorted out their gear and settled down for an uneasy night.

Chapter 12
Pieces On The Board

08:00 sharp everyone was on-air again. Jefferson started. "Bunny. Anything to report?"

Bunny was feeling the strain from a late night. "Yes boss. The network crew at City report hack attempts from somewhere further up North Main. Looks like it's coming from the Military Institute so it could be the robot looking for you. So far they've repelled the attacks but the attempts are getting more sophisticated. I've asked them to let me know if it either stops trying to hack them or succeeds in getting in. The city surveillance systems have turned up no sign of the robot but they only really cover the shopping malls, civic areas and main roads."

Hooper whispered to Smith, "Why would she want to know if it stops?"

Smith turned his head and shared some insight. "It would be a good indicator that the Hydra found another way in to City Hall's network that no one's watching."

Jefferson picked up the thread. "Ok. Hilly, Duds, you know what to do. Get up to that golf course and see if it's there. No weapons, so it doesn't see you as a threat. I'll check in at the top of every hour to spare my battery. Anyone got anything else to say?"

No one could add to the conversation so it came to a natural end. Duds and Hilly geared up for a gentle morning ride up-town on the comfy Suzuki.

Hawkeye stayed on the sofa rubbing liniment into his aching hip. He could use the enforced sofa time to study the maps a little more. Bunny turned back to the console and monitored the relative silence while giving her rabbit's ear some serious worrying; and struggled to ignore the stench of the liniment.

Duds brought the bike steadily in on Second Street. There was no rush so they took their time to take a look at what was rapidly becoming a ghost town. Hardly any activity. People had certainly been scared off by what had happened but there was still the odd truck running around. The die-hards no doubt, who would have the deeds to their property taken from their cold, dead, clammy hands. He turned north onto Main, passing the widely spaced buildings with their large car parks. Even here there wasn't much human activity. The morning after a scare was usually when the pulse of life tried to start beating again, but apparently not this morning. A sense of foreboding still hung in the air. What was left of the population was still being cautious.

The concrete buildings gave way to the tree lined section that led up to the Institute and the golf course. Hilly tapped Duds on the shoulder and pointed to the club house as they passed it, but they rode on further and parked up a respectable distance away. Getting off the bike and taking it slowly, they advanced carefully; creeping around the trees until they could see the golf carts parked outside. There on the end of the row, was the Hydra. Its battleship grey body stood out like a sore thumb.

"It's still unpacked." Duds observed, whispering.

Hilly took a look through the binoculars. "It's got its back to us. Looks like Hawkeye ripped a section of the neck out." She zoomed in a little and inspected the body. "The damage is stopping it from folding itself back down. I can see marks on the body paint where it's been trying." She handed the bins to Duds and checked her watch. "Got another half hour before the next call in."

"That looks like a reasonable sized hole. You reckon we should get Hawkeye up here to finish it off where it stands?"

"Possibly. No point if it could see him coming though."

"How would it do that?"

"Not sure. You were the one that spent the time with their techies. Didn't they tell you anything about how far those sensors on its head can see?"

"No. We just went in to how much punishment it could take." Duds put down the binoculars. "I haven't got a clue how we're going to take that thing down if we can't get close."

"You think there's mileage in getting it to the same spot as before?"

"Nope. If that thing's running a learning game then it'll be wary of the centre of town." Duds paused and looked at the ground for a moment. He decided to tackle Hilly on another subject. "You know, Hawkeye said that you weren't quite yourself. He said that you started behaving a bit odd after we saw that robot in action, and you got worse after the church thing. Are you OK?"

Hilly sighed. She'd been found out but she tried to continue the deception. "Yes, I'm fine."

He kept his voice cool and concerned. "No you're not. You're detached. There's something on your mind and we need you in the game."

They stood there for a while. Duds gave her a bit of time to open up to him. Finally, she did. "It's just so cold."

Duds thought for a moment. "You're not talking about the weather, right?"

"No. I'm talking about that thing." she nodded at the Hydra.

He sighed. "We kill people for a living. Not only that but we get up close and personal about it. But you're getting upset over a bundle of electronics and motors. I don't get it."

Hilly looked him in the eyes. "The people we kill are monsters. It's them or us. They'd be all to happy to walk over everything I am and what I stand for. They hate me, I hate them. Nothing wrong with a bit of mutual one on one. I've got a good reason to fight those nutters."

"But not this."

"No. Not this. That thing is a level of cold calculating monster that I've never dealt with before."

They stood there watching it for a while. Occasionally Duds brought the binoculars up to his eyes again but there was no movement from it. Finally he ventured an opinion. "You think we should get the hell out of here?"

"Yes. Come on, lets go."

They turned around to go back to the bike only to find themselves staring face to face with the drone. It's neck was extended and the barrel was pointed at Hilly. They froze on the spot. Where the hell had it come from?

"I didn't hear that thing coming." She said.

"Neither did I."

"Do you think its gonna shoot us?"

"Nah. If it was going to do that, it would have done it already." They took a moment to think. The drone didn't even flinch. It was as cold and unmoving as the Hydra itself. "Let's just work our way slowly back to the bike."

Very carefully, keeping their eyes on the drone, they walked sideways around it. As they moved, it turned to face them and when they started walking backwards it moved forward to match. It always maintained the same distance and always remained pointing its barrel at Hilly. "I guess we'd better not talk but just get on the bike and ride." Duds opined glancing occasionally over his shoulder to see where they were going.

"I reckon you're right." said Hilly with a slight quiver in her voice and her eyes fixed on the gun barrel of the drone. Part of her wished that she had at least attempted to whack seven bells out of the damn thing in the church, but with the gun barrel pointing directly at her, she kept her cool and let Duds lead the way back to the bike.

When they got to the Suzuki he tapped her hip and she awkwardly swung her leg over the seat, never once taking her eyes off the drone. With her safely on, Duds mounted the bike, kicked the engine in to action and in a well practised movement, knocked the stand away and revved them out of there in double quick time.

He decided to take them north and when they were a reasonable way out, worked his way anti-clockwise around the edge of town. Neither of them said a word but Hilly was looking over her shoulder every few seconds. By the time they had circled the roads and hit Second Street, they concluded that they weren't being followed. Their heads said that they'd had a lucky escape, but their nervous systems were telling them something different; and experience had told them to trust their intuition. It was also the top of the hour so they turned on their radios and joined the banter.

The situation as a whole didn't look good. Bunny and Hawkeye were in the RV in the fields well out to the east of town. Duds and Hilly were on the edge of the west side. Jefferson was somewhere in hiding to the north and the robot was roughly between the lot of them. They were split up with no plan and to make it worse Duds and Hilly felt naked without any weapons.

"Anything to report?" asked Jefferson.

Duds broke the news, as Hilly was still shaking off the last bits of shock. "Well, it's there all right. It has its drone running patrol. Looks like Hawkeye's shot opened up its neck a bit and it can't turn itself flat any more. General, can your drones pick it up again?"

"Sure. I'll have them home in on it now."

At her station, Bunny had the benefit of using an actual headset as opposed to an earpiece, so she heard the subtle tone in Duds' voice. "There's more, isn't there."

"Yup. While we were watching the big guy, the

143

drone was watching us. It could have taken us both out easily but it didn't. It actually followed us until we rode out of there. Spooked the heck out of Hilly 'cause she couldn't work out what was going on in its microchip skull, and I can't say I blame her."

Bunny instantly asked what everyone was thinking. "Did it follow you?"

"Don't think so but I wouldn't like to... hang on." Duds checked the back of the bike. "Hell. A tracker." He ripped the tracking device off the bike and started to smash it under the heel of his riding boot, but Hilly stopped him before he managed to break it.

Smith elbowed in to the conversation. "I think it is safe to assume that it knows you're pieces on the chess board now."

Jefferson added, "It was probably hoping that you'd lead it to me."

Hilly, wide eyed, summed up the situation. "I think we should move. Now. West; further out of town." Duds didn't question her. He hopped on the bike and started the engine while Hilly mounted up behind him. As Duds opened up the throttle and took them away from town at speed, Hilly spoke again over the roar of the engine. "Bunny, if you're in the city's camera system is there one looking where we just were at?"

"Yes. You were on a major road. Hang on." Just as she started switching through the CCTV cameras an e-mail came in. The network crew at City Hall had a message. They said that the Hydra had stopped trying to attack the surveillance systems. "The robot stopped hacking. No clue why yet." She hit a few buttons and switched through the cameras until she found the one covering the main approach road from the reservation. As she watched the now empty tarmac, the Hydra appeared and examined the tracker on the floor. "Looks like you made it out just in time. If you'd smashed the tracker then the damn robot might have made an effort to get to you sooner."

Jefferson started to worry. He hated it when his team were in danger. "Is it following them?"

"No, I think Duds got away in time. I think it's calculating its next move. General, we need to redirect the drones. The Hydra's on West Second in plain sight."

"OK."

Bunny looked at one of her other monitors. The robot still wasn't talking with the mainframe. It obviously still thought it had all the information it needed. She picked up her rabbit from the console, put it in her lap, leant back and tugged at its ears harder than ever before. A slight ping sounded as some of the stitches gave way. There was one more possibility why the robot wasn't using the mainframe. It might have another source of information. As she sat there fretting at the fluffy ears, she was transfixed by the robot on the monitor. It was just sitting there. Another e-mail came in. Apparently news of the failure yesterday had led even more people to leave town. City Hall guessed that less than a tenth of the population was left and those that were still there were staying at home. That explained why the roads were so empty.

It was almost as if the robot had proclaimed

itself the new ruler of Roswell. The more she stared at it, the more she started to understand what Hilly was feeling. Cold, indifferent, logical; the worst opponent they could possibly face. On the edge of her conscience she heard an announcement over the radio that the drones had picked up their target and that a rolling duty had been set up so that they shouldn't lose sight of it again; at least until nightfall.

On the sofa Hawkeye groaned. "Earth to Bunny. Earth to Bunny. Come in Bunny."

"Sorry. Just trying to think." said Bunny not taking her eyes off the monitor.

Hawkeye nudged himself up a little and took a look at what she was staring at on the screen. "Scary, isn't it."

"Yup."

They fell in to silence again.

Jefferson sat alone in the treatment plant. He knew that the chain link fence around it would offer him no protection. It would simply be an early warning if the robot came for him. Not much of an early warning but it was better than nothing. The floor was covered in pebbles and he was absent mindedly picking them up and throwing them at the concrete sides of the large, circular treatment containers. His team was now spread out and they didn't have a plan. This wasn't how things were supposed to be.

Meanwhile Duds and Hilly had reached the Mescalero community centre. Hooper was talking with the Tribal Council over the phone. The two of them were feeling disconnected. Duds could see

Hilly mentally going into herself. It was as if the unfeeling, logical chill of their enemy was starting to reach into her chest and turn her heart as cold as its thick, metal hide. He put his arm around her shoulder and rocked her gently towards him in comfort. "Don't worry. We'll think of something."

She turned her head and spoke. "What the hell are we realistically able to do against this thing? Have we actually got to wait until everyone has left town so we can nuke the place?" In the depth of her eyes Duds saw the shadow of loss, defeat and hopelessness. It made him sad and hurt to see her like this.

Duds lowered his head. "There's something we can do. I don't know what but ... something. We just haven't thought of it yet."

That was how the two of them remained; Duds comforting Hilly, gently rocking her and feeding her small talk while time passed.

Chapter 13
On The Beach

In operations, Smith and Hooper were feeling the same sense of defeat as Jefferson's team. The main screen was showing an echo of what Bunny was seeing. The robot defiantly sat on West Second not caring about the drones hovering above it.

"I can't take much more of this." said Smith. He reached to his side for another doughnut but the desk was empty except for a circular stain of fat. "Damn." He got up and looked at Hooper. "I'm..."

"Off to the doughnut machine." He finished Smith's sentence with a casual air of familiarity.

"You know me too well." Smith threw a casual semi-smile at Hooper who just shook his head and let Smith walk out the door to make the routine walk to the vending area.

He didn't walk very quickly. There was no need to hurry. They were out of ideas and out of hope. The familiar blue carpet complete with wear marks, comforted his mind. It exuded a tone of warmth and intimacy that helped him feel that somehow, things weren't as bad as they seemed. When he rounded the corner there was his favourite machine, stood there just as it always had done. His rock. His comfort. His emotional blanket.

He walked over to the glass panel and looked in at the treats for sale. His coffee favourites had run out and he was now working his way through the toffee. They were probably starting to run low as well. He ran his hand over the back of his neck to try and help with the tension he was feeling and in the process he absent mindedly tilted his head back. He found himself looking up at the banana slot only to find that they had been replaced with a row of maple glazed bacon. "Oh, that's just taking the piss." he said to no one in particular. Obviously his interfering hadn't gone down well with the doughnut company. Well, so long as they kept feeding him coffee glaze ring, he'd survive.

As he stood there staring at the machine, he realised that he wasn't feeling quite right. Had he eaten too many doughnuts? No, that wasn't it. Had too much walking to the vending machines caused him to over exercise? Nope, that wasn't the cause either. A bit of soul searching revealed that he was suffering the symptoms of failure coupled with the realisation of hopelessness. As a result his stomach felt like he'd eaten concrete for breakfast, his heart felt like it was pumping molten lead around his body and his brain felt like it was lost in a giant maze with no stars or sun with which to navigate by.

His body was reporting that it was fed up with being depressed and powerless so it wanted to just eat itself in to pleasurable oblivion.

'I'm not actually hungry.' he told his brain.

'That's got nothing to do with it.' his brain replied.

'If I'm not hungry, then why do you want me to stuff my face?' he queried, not wanting to admit defeat too easily.

'Because it will make me feel good.' it spat back at him.

'But that won't change anything.'

'Yes it will. I'll feel good.'

'Only for a short time. All it will do is make me fat and then I'll feel worse.'

'Deal with that problem later. Just buy the damn doughnuts.'

'No.'

'Yes.'

'No.'

'If you don't then I'll go off in a huff.' his brain threatened.

Smith stepped back from the machine and considered his options. He needed to think and behind him was a bank of nondescript waiting room chairs that lined one wall of the refreshment area. He slumped down on to one of them and put his head in his hands. Never mind winning a battle with a robot. He couldn't even beat his own brain in a fair fight.

Someone had left a newspaper on the next chair over. He glanced at the headlines to distract him from his internal battle. The usual garbage. The UK Prime Minister was talking rubbish about censoring the internet and banning encryption. 'Honestly,' he thought, 'why did the Brits keep electing idiots like that to run the country; premiers who couldn't even be bothered to take basic technological advice before spouting utter nonsense.' His memory then recalled some of the presidents that had been ensconced in the White House in recent decades, and effectively answered his own question.

There was an article about forest fires and a picture of a lone helicopter trying desperately to battle a massive fire raging beneath it. 'David against Goliath.' he thought to himself. 'Are we really coming up to that season already?' Then a piece about Richmond, California, caught his eye. Apparently they were paying criminals up to a thousand bucks a month not to commit any crimes. 'Bloody hell.' he thought. 'Perhaps I'm in the wrong job.'

He picked up the paper and read the article. As usual, it turned out to be somewhat different than what the headline suggested. The payments were only for a short period and were aimed at giving people a breathing space. Instead of using all their energy to fight for survival, this allowed them the chance to build themselves a platform from which they could make a better future for themselves. It was apparently yielding good results. Not a hundred percent but it was good enough to make a worthwhile difference.

Smith put the paper down and considered whether they could pay the robot not to be any trouble. Then again, he thought, what would the thing spend the money on? A new paint job? Flame decals? Perhaps it would fit itself with a radio and get some hydraulics fitted to its wheels. Then it could hang a fluffy dice from its neck and bounce itself down the road to the tunes of some rap artist or other. Now that would be a sight. Cruising lights maybe? Perhaps it would take up dancing. Well, at least it could do a very convincing, 'robot.'

He got up and returned to the machine. Folding his arms in front of his chest, he leant his forehead on the glass. Boston Cream sounded nice. Perhaps cinnamon? Hmmm......

As one part of his mind was running over the choices, another part of his mind was recalling the previous radio conversations.

He heard the ghost of Hawkeye's voice crossing his thoughts, *"I'm pretty sure I did open up a gap on the back of its neck, though."* The distant, gentle voice changed to Hilly's stressed observation, *"What do you want us to do? Tell it that it looks a bit dirty, offer it a free car wash and hope it shorts itself?"*

He tapped the glass with his fingers. There was something he was missing. Something which was just on the edge of his grasp. All of a sudden, he snapped his body straight and screamed, "Of course!" He made a dive for the newspaper. Snatching it off the seat he turned and raced back to the operations room. The poor, sleepy, deflated souls that occupied ops, jumped out of their skins as he smashed through the doors.

"Here!" he said, short of breath, slamming the paper down in front of Hooper.

"What?"

Smith was in a frenzy. He was hopping up and down jabbing at the paper with his finger. "This! Robot! Neck! Water!"

Hooper took a look at the paper and connected with the image of the helicopter fighting the forest fire. "Damn!" He stood up and grabbed the over excited Smith by the shoulders. "You're a bloody genius!" He turned to the Signals soldier. "Get me as many fire fighting helicopters and planes as you can in the Roswell area. I want them to fill up with water and drop their loads on that robot. NOW!"

"Sir, it's a desert area. There's not much forest to catch fire."

"So it'll take them a little longer to get there. Do I have to think of everything? Just do it."

"Yes, sir!"

Hooper jumped on the radio. "Jefferson. You there?"

"The boss isn't but I am Sir." came Bunny.

"We've got a plan. Hang tight, we're sending something in. I don't want to say anything more over the radio but you'll know it when you hear it. Um, eventually."

Hilly, Duds and Hawkeye were all listening in, and a tiny spark of hope fired up in their chests. Perhaps there was a way to defeat this thing after all.

Hooper turned to the Signals soldier again. "Get drones in there armed with rockets. If that robot tries to take cover anywhere, blow it back in to the open again. We need to keep hitting it with water. Understood?"

"Yes, sir."

Alarms were sounding at various air fields both in the area and far beyond. The instruction to send air borne fire fighting equipment in to the desert seemed more than a little odd; but they responded, nonetheless. It was going to take a little time to get the different aircraft ready to drop water but they snapped into action. While they worked, time ticked long in Arizona and breath remained bated in both Roswell and the reservation. In the last few days, Hooper had issued several orders that, on the face of it, made it sound like he had gone utterly mad; but he was starting to get used to the feeling.

For its part the Hydra wasn't moving. It obviously didn't have anywhere it felt it needed to go. Perhaps there weren't any valid moves for it to make and it was waiting for someone else to do something. There was no way to tell what was going on in its electronic brain.

Duds and Hilly were still in the reservation Community Centre. There was a bit of a bustle around them as Hooper's phone call had obviously caused concern, but they didn't know what had been said so they played dumb. People seemed torn. The thing was obviously powerful enough to be causing the military trouble so what was to be gained by them joining in? Others were speaking of duty, that they were too close to just sit there and do nothing. The discussion was going around in circles with no easy end in sight.

"I don't like not knowing what's going on around me." Duds admitted.

"Well as long as they're not looking to us for any answers I guess we're off the hook." Hilly was starting to get a grip on her emotions but without an actual game plan she was kicking her heels and she didn't like that; unless of course there was beer to drink and a TV not to watch.

They sat there for a while longer. No one was raising their voices but likewise no one had asked them to clarify anything either. A few people had looked at them pointedly during some closed conversations but that was understandable.

Duds couldn't take much more. "I'm going outside."

"I'll join you."

They left and returned to Duds' bike.

"So what *are* we going to do?" prompted Hilly.

"I don't know. I just still don't know." As they stood there an aeroplane went overhead, followed in short order by two large helicopters. "Bugger. Those things are carrying Bambi Buckets."

"Water."

"Probably going to try and drench the robots neck."

"Dare we follow them without weapons?"

"Nah if this doesn't work then we'd be walking into certain death. That would make us no use to anyone."

Hilly kicked some stones on the ground. "I hope this works. This is the most spooked I've ever been about a mission."

While the aircraft converged on Roswell, the top of another hour hit and it was radio time once more.

"Has everybody heard the engines?" Jefferson queried.

"Yup, couldn't miss them." Bunny put forward. "You were off air when Hooper said they had an idea."

"Same here. Aircraft overhead. I think what they're doing is a long shot but it's something." added Hilly.

"OK. Well if we don't know what the result might be, we're going to have to assume that there's going to be some mopping up to do. Hawkeye, have you got any transport?"

Hawkeye shrugged his shoulders so Bunny had

to answer, "We've got a little moped stored in the RV. Only really any good for running around a camp site."

"That'll have to do. Take that into town and see what you can do. An incendiary round down that neck hole is possibly the last chance we've got if Hooper's plan fails. Remember it's still got one rocket on board. Bunny, keep a track of what happens and keep Hawkeye up to date. My radio is nearly dead so I'm going to have a decision to make shortly."

"Yes boss." said Bunny, as Hawkeye got off the sofa as quickly as his pained hip would allow. Limping around to his secure cabinet, Hawkeye opened his bank of drawers. There was an empty space where the Windrunner used to be and it cheated him of a bit of that, 'Everything's gonna be OK,' sort of feeling. The fact that the gun was absent enforced in his mind that they were already starting from a heavily disadvantaged position. This time they really were up against the odds. He took out the CheyTac and went to the second drawer for some incendiary rounds as well as some standard, armour-piercing ammo. With that done he grabbed a pair of binoculars and made himself busy unpacking the moped out of its odd little compartment in the RV.

While he was doing that, the battle of West Second had begun. The robot initially didn't think anything of the approaching aircraft. When one of them dumped its load of water right on top of it however, the robot's opinion changed and it did some calculations. While it was trying to work out what had happened a helicopter scored a direct hit as well.

"Sir." came a voice in ops. "It's asking for detailed maps of the area."

"Stop it." barked Hooper. "It mustn't find any place that could give it cover." The operator made use of the time delay they installed earlier, to kill the information that the mainframe wanted to send to the Hydra. The robot wasn't going to wait around, however. It took off at speed towards the centre of town.

While it was heading east, there was a helicopter heading west. The crew on board made a bit of a guess and succeeded. The Hydra took yet another dousing.

As it was racing forward, its scanners noticed some tin shelters. They were outside an army surplus store, tucked behind a chain link fence. The robot broke through the fence and smashed straight into one of the shelters. There was a clatter and clang as various tools, metal boxes and assorted bits and pieces were thrown into the air, but as far as the robot was concerned it was cover from the water; which is exactly what logic dictated it needed.

Up in the sky a drone had aimed a missile and let it loose. Within a few short seconds the robots relief was torn asunder as the resultant explosion blew a hole in the tarmac and sent all the tin huts in to the air. The Hydra itself was thrown sideways by the impact, but hit the side of the store and managed to stay upright. This forced it to re-evaluate its immediate landscape and calculate a new route. In the seconds that it was taking to do this it was hit with another large dump of water, this time from an aeroplane.

"It's damaged." came a voice in ops.

"Great." shouted Hooper enthusiastically. "How bad?"

"Don't know Sir, I'm trying to decode its reports." While this was going on Smith reached instinctively for a doughnut. He was caught. He forgot to get any while he was at the vending machine and now that there was some positive action happening, he didn't want to tear himself away from the monitors. Damn! The tension inside him was rising, however. He needed a sugar fix and he needed it badly. For a brief moment he even contemplated licking the fat stain on the desk but managed to stop himself. He wasn't that desperate… yet.

The Hydra backed out of the yard negotiating the re-formed landscape and the debris around it, and managed to get back onto Second. It started back along the road into the town centre. Another two helicopters dumped their loads on it before the robot accidentally found cover. It had tried to make the turn from Second to go north on Main but had too much speed. As a result, it smashed through the floor-to-ceiling window of a shop and came to a halt just inside the broken glass.

As it stood there, it detected the radar signature of a missile lock but its systems said there was nothing it could do about it. It didn't have any surface to air missiles left and, being inside the building, its sniper rifle was useless. It's one remaining rocket was also no good against the aircraft. While it was calculating its next move a missile smashed into the floor behind it, throwing the Hydra across the inside of the building; crashing through partition walls. It eventually came to rest against the rear wall of the shop.

The place it had accidentally chosen to hide in, happened to be one of the many alien experience premises that had given Roswell its reputation. Cheap, green, plastic alien masks floated in the air, mingling with shop invoices and leaflets advertising the various extra terrestrial exhibitions in the area.

Just as the building dust was starting to settle, another missile landed. This time it hit the centre of the ceiling and collapsed the entire building. The walls were a ragged mess and the floor sported a very nice crater, but the important thing was that the robot was exposed to the air again and in very short order, a helicopter and an aeroplane dumped their loads on top of it.

"That's it, Sir. All aircraft are empty and are heading home."

Hooper looked at the picture feed from one of the drones. He hoped the shop owner had insurance. In fact, the shops either side were also in bad shape and the windows of several other premises had been blown out from the shock. He looked at the operations terminal that was handling the robot's status. Smith was working with the operative to match the part numbers to the actual limbs and sections on the Hydra's body so that they could interpret the fault codes.

"Not much damage, Sir. It's lost the use of its machine guns and its surface to air mechanisms are jammed. It's also got a problem with elevating the sniper rifle beyond ten degrees. That's it."

"That explains why it didn't shoot back. Did you get that, Jefferson?" barked Hooper.

"Yes, Sir. We need to know where it is now so that Hawkeye can get a second..."

Smith looked at the main monitor to see the drone feeds. "It's heading north again presumably back to the golf course."

Duds chimed in. "Boss, I request that Hilly and I race through town to get back to the RV."

Silence.

Bunny piped up. "I think the boss's radio just gave out. Hilly, effectively you're in command until he gets back in the game."

Finally, there was a sense that they could really beat the thing. Hilly relished the fact that not only were there decisions that could be made but it was now her call to make them. She took charge. "OK, we're coming in. Hawkeye, continue with your last orders. See if you can get a shot at it." They mounted up and Duds rode as fast as he could on Second back into Roswell.

Hawkeye was still phut-phutting his way into town with his rifle slung awkwardly across his back. There were occasional domestic trucks passing him in haste, obviously in the opposite direction. The sound of the missiles going off must have persuaded the last of Roswell's residents to get the heck out of town. "Sure, but this isn't going to be quick." he confirmed on the radio.

The centre of town was going to be a wreck so he went a roundabout way to get on to Main and turned north. If the robot really was, as they suspected, heading back to the golf course then he had to get on to the roof of some of the buildings at the Military Institute to have any chance of a decent shot. While he was on the sofa with his hip in agony, he'd taken a good look at the map. He knew there was a vehicle repair shop at the north west of town, which was close to the course club house. If that damn metal nightmare had, indeed, decided to head for the course then that was the building he needed to get on top of. While he phutted his way up Main he made inpatient, 'gee up,' movements in a vain effort to make the moped go faster.

With Hawkeye heading north, Duds and Hilly were riding into Roswell. They saw the soaked road where the robot had been attacked. A little further down was the wreckage of the missile blast that had taken out the tin sheds and blown the roof off the surplus store. It was a total mess. Duds had to swerve around assorted old ammo boxes, shoes and other items. Part of him wanted to stop and see if there was anything in his size but he pressed on.

When they came across the junction between Second and Main they saw the carnage that the two missiles had visited on the area. There were skid marks showing where the robot had been going too fast to take the corner and that explained why it had gone off the road and into the shops. Duds very carefully negotiated the rubble and picked his way further east to the RV. Behind the bike, plastic alien masks and paperwork fluttered in the air, littering the road and sidewalk.

When they finally pulled up at the RV, Duds

made for the door but Hilly went straight for her weapons stash. Duds tried to stop her. "Boss's orders were no arms."

Hilly had recovered from her sense of helplessness and she was working her way towards a minor rage. "Screw orders. If I'm going in to battle to get shot at by a tin can, I want to be able to shoot back. And he's out of contact so I'm in charge now. Remember?"

"You know we've got nothing that will touch that thing. Standard weapons are useless. Apart from which it won't be that long before the boss finds himself some fresh batteries. It isn't like he's taken a fatal wound or something."

Hilly wasn't listening. She had already opened her drawer in the bottom of the RV and was taking out her long range FN SCAR-H assault rifle. Duds went wide eyed, gulped and retreated in to the RV. Hilly was getting really angry and she was using that to put her, 'in the zone.' Past experience had taught Duds that he didn't want to be anywhere around Hilly when she started seriously tooling up.

"What's the news?" Duds asked of Bunny, who was sat at her control station with the rabbit on her lap. It's ears were taking some serious strain from all the tugging that Bunny was doing. Some of the seams were starting to give way again and one ear was already half off.

"The damage to the Hydra wasn't as much as we'd hoped but it has done something. Hawkeye is making his way into position at the golf course now."

"Is it still trying to get into the surveillance

systems?"

"Good question. I'll find out." Bunny leant forward and tapped out an e-mail to City Hall's network team, then encrypted it and hit the send button.

"Why don't you just call them?"

"They'll have to look through log files and stuff; I'd be hanging on the phone for ages. Also some of the reports aren't easy to read over the phone; they're all numbers and things. Easier for them to just e-mail the files to me."

Duds just shook his head in bewilderment. If it went kaboom he could understand that. All these bits and bytes and things, however, were just not his cup of napalm. His ears pricked when he thought he heard his motocross so he stuck his head out the door. Yes! That was his bike incoming. He glanced to the side and saw Hilly was now sporting a vest loaded with grenades and magazines. She was putting a helmet on and there was a pair of shades in her hand. "Oh god." he said, walking down the stairs. "You're going full Afghanistan on us, aren't you."

"You bet."

"Well, the boss is nearly here so you can explain that to him."

A few moments later, Jefferson rode up and parked in front of Duds. "Battery gave up. No option but to come in." he said while he got off the bike and caught a glimpse of Hilly, standing behind Duds. "Getting a new … what the hell are you doing Barfour? I thought I told you no arms."

"With all due respect, Sir… go to hell."

Jefferson exploded at her, "You don't tell me to go to hell soldier. I'm your commanding officer and you'll do what I damn well tell you. Get those arms off. *Now*."

Hilly stood her ground. "That robot knows that Duds and me are a line to you. We're no longer innocent bystanders that if we don't shoot at it, then it won't shoot at us. So with all due respect Sir, I say again … go to hell." As if to add extra weight to her statement she pulled the rack lever and armed the gun.

Jefferson was furious. It was one of the unique things about their team. They survived purely because they had strong personalities and as such, had each others backs; but their fierce individuality could also set them at each other's throats if they weren't careful. He didn't give a damn that she'd primed the rifle. That didn't threaten him at all. His problem was that she felt like she had to do it and also that she'd disobeyed him directly, twice. Those were the things he had to think on. Why did she feel that strongly and what was he going to do about it? And he only had a matter of moments in which to make that decision.

Duds looked at Jefferson and raised his eyebrows as if to say, 'Let her win this one, boss,' in the hope that he'd take the hint.

They stayed like that for a few moments. A stand off with the ball firmly in Jefferson's court. Eventually, taking a deep breath, he tried reasoning with her. "Look Hilly, the rounds you've got in that thing won't even tickle it. Just what the hell do you expect to achieve?"

"I don't know boss but ever since we had eyeball with that thing, it's scared the crap out of me and now I just want to go in hoping that I can scare the crap out of it."

"It's a machine! You don't scare a computer by waving a gun at it. If such a thing actually worked, then office staff the world over would be licensed to carry firearms. You encounter that thing with nothing in your hands and you stand a chance that it'll leave you breathing, but if it sees you as a threat it'll kill you without a second thought. Because that's exactly the point. It… doesn't… think."

"Then maybe I'm fed up with breathing boss. Scared ain't no way to live or die."

That caught Jefferson right between the eyes. "Damn it, Hilly."

Before he could deliver any form of verdict, Bunny yelled from inside the trailer. "Hawkeye's in position boss."

Jefferson pointed at the FN SCAR. "At least put the safety on." He then jumped in to the RV followed by Duds and, after pushing a small metal lever into position on the rifle, Hilly joined them.

Jefferson handed his radio to Bunny. "Need a new bat in that." She handed him her headset and rose to get a new radio. "OK, Hawkeye, report."

"I'm on the building across from the course and the robot's here. It's actually smashed its way into the club house so it's under cover. I just haven't got a clean shot at the neck."

"Hooper, do you think it's worth sending in another missile to blow it into the open?"

In ops, Hooper and Smith looked at each other

as if they were exchanging thoughts by telepathy. After a short while, Hooper keyed the mike. "No. By the time that the aircraft refill and get back to Roswell again it will be too dark to safely target the thing with Hawkeye nearby. Too risky. At least we know where it is now so we can wait until morning."

Bunny handed another radio to Jefferson and took back her headset. He stood there for a short while considering the options while he fitted the fresh radio in his ear. Eventually he spoke. "OK, Hilly and Duds, I want you out with Hawkeye. If that thing shifts you track it by bike. Now, if..."

"Boss," crackled Hawkeye over the radio. "I've spotted the drone rolling around the golf course. Permission to take it out?"

Just as Jefferson thought he had a plan, he switched gear and re-thought it. "OK, you shoot the drone. Duds, get to the ambush site and rescue some of those explosives. Hilly, you're with me and we'll join Hawkeye. OK people, let's go."

"Wait!" yelled Bunny. She went into the back and returned with a bright pink balaclava. "Take this boss."

"What? Why?"

"You're heading into town and if that thing has access to the cameras, it will see you and come running."

"Good point." Jefferson took the balaclava and reluctantly put it on his head. Hilly and Duds had a small chuckle and even Bunny smiled. "Well it's not as if there's anyone in Roswell to see me like this. Come on, let's go." One day, he would have to sit down with Bunny to find out what it was with her and pink. As a last action he grabbed some binoculars and power bars, and then headed out the door.

Second Street had been shocked into silence. There wasn't even bird song. It was the kind of quiet that sets your nerves completely on edge. Here and there were clumps of papers, leaflets and plastic alien masks. Some of them were resting while others jumped the occasional foot or two as gusts of wind came along to aid their escape. A few moments later, however, that silence was shattered by the roar of Duds' Suzuki and the whine of the motocross as the three of them made their way back in to town again.

Chapter 14
The Queen

The roads in town were so bad that when they hit the junction of Second and Main, Duds' Suzuki couldn't turn north over the piles of debris. They had to continue a little further before they could change direction. There were piles of bricks and shattered glass everywhere. Missiles were always a very messy way of dealing with things.

They didn't have far to ride up Richardson before they reached the place where they had laid the first ambush. Duds peeled off to deal with the explosives while Jefferson drove Hilly and himself up to the repair shop that Hawkeye was camped on.

In the mean time, Hawkeye had one of the drone's wheels in his sights. They hadn't test fired at the drone in the AMARS labs but Hicks had mentioned that they weren't anywhere near as tough as the Hydra itself. He should be able to get off a round at the drone and duck down before the robot would know he was there. He watched and waited for the drone to stop and perform a turn.

Back in the RV Bunny got a response to her e-mail. No, the robot wasn't hacking the firewall any more because it was already in the surveillance system. As she read the report it was obvious what had happened. Some of the CCTV cameras were wireless and that included units installed in parts of the Institute. The short range wireless cameras were an easier hacking target than going in through the front door firewalls. They had a very limited radio range but they were far, far easier for the robot to break into.

Bunny stopped worrying the rabbits ears; but that was only because she now gripped them tightly. It explained perfectly why the robot had gone back there. It needed to be there so it could connect to the wireless network and use the cameras to watch them. And that's exactly what it was doing now. It was watching them, while they were watching it.

Hawkeye hadn't paid any attention to the security tower which was off to his right hand side. If he had given it the once over, then he might have seen that there was a CCTV camera on top of it and that it was pointing at him.

BANG went the CheyTac as it buried itself into his shoulder. The incendiary round went straight into the drone's wheel and stopped it dead.

BANG went a piece of wall right underneath Hawkeye's face. He looked back at the Hydra and found that he was staring straight down the barrel of its sniper rifle. He nearly soiled his trousers right then.

BANG went a second round, again eating in to the wall beneath him, and this time he saw the empty shell fly out from the robot's shoulder.

Hawkeye went in to a mild rage. Any sense of self preservation left him and all he wanted to do now was kill the drone. "Shoot at me would you, you bastard? Well, I'll teach you and your little wheeled buddy." He shouldered the CheyTac again, lifted the bolt and pulled it back. The spent cartridge spun gracefully out of the breach and tinkled onto the roof beside him. He pushed the bolt back home, sucking up another round from the magazine in the process, and secured the lever in position.

He took aim once more at the drone. BANG went the CheyTac. BANG went the wall beneath him. "Kerklack," went the bolt and another case flew into the air as another fresh round went in to position in the breach. BANG ... another round went straight into the body of the drone, this time causing it to explode. "Yes! Eat that you bastard." BANG ... the wall beneath his face was almost gone.

Hawkeye spun his rifle round to start shooting at the Hydra itself, but at that very moment he felt something grip his ankles and he was bodily pulled back from the edge. He turned over and took a look through his legs to see that a pink hooded Jefferson had stopped his play time. He was flat on his stomach, along with Hilly who also had her head down. Jefferson yelled at him, "Are you suicidal, soldier?"

"No Sir," managed Hawkeye through gritted teeth, actually shaking a little with adrenaline and anger from the sniper-to-sniper fire fight. "Just a bit tense, that's all Sir!"

"Damn it man, if that robots sniper rifle wasn't faulty you'd be pushing up daisies. Just one more degree of elevation and it would have been your skull that got shot to hell. Couldn't you have been a little more tactical about taking the bloody drone out?"

The radio crackled. It was Bunny. "Boss, the robot *has* got in to the surveillance system, by hacking the wireless cameras."

While Jefferson and Hawkeye were still locked eye to eye via the bulge of Hawkeye's manhood, Hilly took a look around them without raising her head, and spotted the lone guard tower. She didn't even need her binoculars to make out the camera looking straight back at them. "Boss, camera on us. Three o'clock." She pointed.

Jefferson broke away from his staring contest with Hawkeye's trousers and followed her arm. "Take it out."

"With pleasure, Sir!" Hilly flipped the assault rifle in to single shot mode, took careful aim and blew it to pieces.

"Can you see the base station it was connecting to?"

Hilly scanned the walls of the buildings. She was looking for anywhere that she thought would be a prime place for someone to put an external wi-fi access point. She spotted a box and took a look through the binoculars. "Got it."

"Take it out."

"No problem." One shot later and it was nothing more than a shadow on the wall, with a wire dangling freely in the wind.

Jefferson breathed a sigh of relief. Hawkeye was coming down nicely from his little jaunt in to la-la land. Their nerves started to loosen a little.

Hilly received an urgent e-mail in the RV and called it over the radio. "Boss, City Hall reports the robot just dropped off the network."

"Not a problem. I think we just revoked its password."

"Oh no. The mainframe just lit up." added

Bunny. "It's asking for something I can't read. It's in code. Smith, can you figure out what it's asking for?"

Back at ops, Smith confirmed, "We can, but it will take a while to decode the numbers. It's also getting dark and the drones are having problems seeing, so we're sending them back to base to refuel."

Bunny started bouncing up and down on her chair in nervous panic. "Shit, shit, shit." she said to herself in rapid succession. After all this silence, there was now a lot of communication going on and she couldn't decipher any of it. Not only that but the eyes in the sky were about to go dark.

Dusk ruled the horizon. Duds was still disassembling the trap they had set. Around him, green plastic alien masks were blowing on the growing wind and it was starting to get chilly. Bunny was stuck in the RV watching the incomprehensible chatter between the robot and the mainframe. Hawkeye, Hilly and Jefferson stayed on the roof maintaining a watch on the Hydra and keeping each other company as the temperature started to fall.

Now that the drones had gone back to their base and the vast majority of Roswell's population had run for the hills, the whole place was eerily silent. That didn't change much on the roof either, where all three of them found that they had very little to say, partly because they couldn't actually believe the situation that they had found themselves in.

Back in operations, they thought they had a lead. "Sir," the operative said to Smith. "It looks like there are two different activities going on in the one stream."

"Ok, what are they?"

"One of them is an analysis of Jefferson's teams radio. It hasn't broken the encryption but it's been trying. It does know their frequencies though and it's been monitoring their positions."

"OK, what's the other stream?"

"It's been sort of playing chess games with the mainframe."

"What?!"

"Yes, Sir. Chess games, but on a battlefield."

"Explain."

"Well, sort of running military strategies but with chess pieces instead of troops."

"Why? What's it's aim?"

"Can't really work it out, Sir. It just doesn't make sense."

Smith looked at Hooper and shrugged his shoulders. Hooper had overheard everything but there was no ray of enlightenment showing on his face either.

Time ticked on. Dusk went to black. Every few minutes, one of the three stuck their heads up to check on the robot. It was still there, holed up in the shelter it had made in the club house.

In Arizona, there was finally something to report. The operatives voice was a bit hesitant and uncertain but he piped up. "I think I'm starting to get a grip on what it's doing, Sir."

"Well, spit it out." Hooper stuck his head into the conversation.

"The strategies it's running. It seems to be

focused on attacking the queen, Sir."

"The queen?" Hooper queried.

"The most powerful piece on the board." Smith interjected.

"Yes, I know that. But what does it mean in our world?" Hooper replied.

"I haven't got a clue Sir." said the operative.

Hooper worried his chin.

Jefferson came over the radio. "The Hydra's gone. Didn't see or hear it go. One moment it was there and the next it was an empty hole. Anyone got any ideas?"

Smith joined in. "None. We can't see it from here. Do you know how much of a head start it's got?"

"Could be three or four minute clear."

Bunny piped up. "I'm cycling through the cameras now. It'll take time."

Hooper started pacing the room, postulating. "Ok, so if Jefferson is the king, then who's the queen? Who is it, that can move to most places on the board in an instant and can protect all the pieces?"

Smith, "Well, Bunny can't move but she does keep them all talking together."

"Information. The organising agent." Hooper lurched forward to the radio. "Bunny! Get out of there!"

"Sorry Sir?"

"Get the hell out of there. It's coming for you."

"I don't..." The beginning part of a loud explosion was heard over the radio.

"Bunny?"

174

Static.

"BUNNY!"

Static.

"Hell. It took out Bunny." he keyed the mike again. "Jefferson, it's got Bunny."

More static.

"Jefferson?"

Smith put his hand on Hooper's shoulder. "Bunny's RV was relaying between us all. With that down we can't talk with Jefferson and they can't talk with each other, either."

"Damn it. We need to get a communication drone in the air. That isn't run of the mill comms gear they're using. And we're going to have to wait for daybreak before we can try and find that damn robot again. Do we have any idea where it could be?"

"I think it will go for the king." said Smith. "Even if it can't get to him, it probably knows his location. Or if not, it can have a damn good guess."

Chapter 15
The King

It was morning and Dudman rode slowly up to the charred wreckage of the RV. Last night, Hooper's warning and Bunny's cut-off response had been the last thing he heard on the radio before it stopped working. He had ceased what he was doing and bedded down for the night in the Wells Fargo building. Bright and early he had gone to the roof to see if the Hydra was anywhere within sight and it wasn't, so he went to an abandoned fuel station, filled up the bike and then rode slowly to where the RV had been parked. He wasn't in a particular rush to get to it, but he knew that he had to go back. Call it finding peace, call it saying goodbye, he didn't know the reason; he just knew that he had to be there.

He brought the Suzuki to a halt just outside the large, oval area of blackened earth. In the middle was a big crater. There was no way that Bunny could have survived that. The only consoling thought was that at least she didn't suffer. There were tinges of both guilt and relief that they kept most of their ordnance in the RV. Without them, there was a slight chance that Bunny might have survived. Actually, Duds corrected himself, with the rocket that the Hydra had thrown at her, the more realistic outcome was that she would have had a slightly slower death by a fraction of milliseconds.

He stopped the engine, kicked out the stand and took his helmet off. Duds waited there for a few moments before he dismounted and walked in to the charred remains that had been the RV. His heart sank to the bottom of his big, bad, biker boots and a tear rolled down his cheek. There was a tightness in his chest and an ache that he couldn't physically account for. As he stood there, another couple of tears followed the first down his face.

He took a few steps around the charred soil. None of them had seen this coming. None of them had even entertained it as a possibility that Bunny could be a target for the robot. It just seemed so … so … well, looking at it now it actually did seem logical. She was the piece that kept them all working as a team. It was common sense that the robot would see her as an important piece to be taken off the board. How the hell could they have let this happen? How didn't they see this coming?

As he took gentle steps among the remains, something pink tugged at the corner of his eye. It was over in the grass a fair distance away. He raised his head and walked over to it. As he approached, it was as he suspected. Bunny's fluffy rabbit. Burned in places, sure, and missing an arm and an ear but otherwise mostly intact. He held it gently and lightly stroked its one remaining ear. His mind knew he was going to miss Bunny, but his heart still didn't know she was gone.

After a few more tears had fallen he turned and went back to his bike. He stuffed the rabbit into one of his saddle bags, put his helmet back on and mounted up. However, he didn't immediately start the engine. He just surveyed the scene once more and said to no one, "Don't worry. I'll make sure that fucking robot pays for this."

Finally, he started the engine, kicked away the stand and rode back into town to finish the job of dismantling the explosives. At least Jefferson would know where to find him.

On the roof at the vehicle shop, silence had reigned throughout the night. Even with the Hydra gone they somehow didn't have the energy or impetus to move. There wasn't really anywhere they could go. They sat there throughout, not really able to sleep. It was almost as if they were actively trying to avoid sleeping because they knew that their minds would dream of Bunny and relive operations they'd been on, beers they'd shared and the occasions they'd been bollocked together, by some commander or other, for misbehaviour on base. Oh yes, those were the good times.

Hilly broke the silence. "Of all of us that should have gone first, it shouldn't have been her."

After the comment gently settled, Hawkeye brought his own observation to the table. "You know, she really cared for us. That poor rabbit's ears never got much peace when we were on ops."

Hilly smiled. "Yeah, the number of times I had to stitch those damn ears back on. She could handle a soldering iron but give her a needle and there'd be more blood on the damn rabbit than there was in her body."

Some random note of desperation hit Hawkeye from somewhere. "You know, we really don't know she'd dead. There..."

Jefferson cut him off. "Stop it. Our radios haven't worked all night. The RV getting blown up is the only explanation and we all know that Bunny was in it at the time." he paused for a moment. "She's gone." He worried the pink balaclava in his hands almost like Bunny tugged at her rabbit's ears. Now it was all that was left of their much loved colleague.

Hawkeye bowed his head and slowly wept. Hilly gripped her rifle a little more tightly and shed a few tears also. Jefferson returned to his uneasy silence; he felt responsible for not seeing this coming.

In operations, they had been up all night. Hooper had run Signals ragged to get some equipment that would get the ground team's radios working again. State of the art kit was great but when it went wrong it was a whole heap of trouble to put right. On top of the equipment itself, the encryption code for their sets had to be hunted down. Then it had to be hooked up to another unit that would link the local radios back into the wider band again and all that, in turn, had to be bundled into a drone and sent into the area.

It was a butt load of work and they were doing it at night which meant people all over the region had to be roused from their bunks and pressed, bleary eyed, into service. However, for all the chaos they had caused on various bases, once people were told exactly which unit was in trouble and why, it was quickly followed by an order for strong coffee, lots of it, and the lights in workshops shone throughout the night.

The moment it was light, Hooper had the drones back in the air again to look for the Hydra.

At about 09:30, he got news that a drone with the communication equipment was airborne and would be over Roswell at roughly 11:00. They watched everything on the monitors.

The first thing they saw was the location of the RV. The degree of the explosion was comforting. The robot had, mercifully, been quick and effective. Then Hooper commanded a drone to the golf course to see if they could pick up a visual of Jefferson and the team.

It would be a short while before the drones were in position so Smith announced, "I'm going..."

"To get more doughnuts. I know." interjected Hooper. "I think I'll come with you." That blind-sided Smith. He normally used the doughnut journey to spend a little time on his own, so having a companion on this trip would be a different experience.

They walked out of operations together. "This way." signalled Smith as he led them along the blue carpet.

"So, Smith. You ever thought about a career in the military?"

"Nope."

His straight and immediate answer puzzled Hooper. "Why not?"

"Your canteens don't seem to carry doughnuts."

Hooper chuckled. "Well, the Pentagon's got two café's, some vending machines and they get pizza delivered. I'm sure they have doughnuts worked into the mix somewhere."

Smith stopped walking and stared at Hooper. "Do they do one covered with maple glazed bacon?"

That caught Hooper completely by surprise. He shrugged his shoulders "Well, I guess they could do one. This is D.C. we're talking about."

Smith started walking again. "If they actually do one of those inhuman concoctions then I'm not interested." he delivered with a straight face.

Hooper just shook his head in bewilderment and started walking again. "Look, you've handled yourself in there with serious class."

"We train for it. It's my job, tracking deadly robots and keeping them in order. We've got some of the most dangerous mechanical entities in the whole damn country. But the way I hear it, Washington's got some of its own heartless monsters that are even more dangerous than the stuff we make here."

"Really?" Hooper was surprised at this. "I've never heard of them. What are they?"

"I think they call them, 'divorce lawyers.'" Smith said; again with a totally dead pan delivery.

Hooper stopped for a moment and put his hands in his pockets. He stared at the back of Smith's head as he continued to walk away. He wasn't totally sure whether Smith was being funny or deadly serious. Perhaps there was a painful divorce in Smith's past. 'Yes.' Hooper thought to himself. 'That would explain a few things.' He vowed to himself that once things had settled down that he would look more closely in to Smith's background.

Sensing that he'd left Hooper behind, Smith stopped and turned around. He continued his line of thinking. "You know, somehow, despite their legendary status in D.C. I think that even I'd get jailed if I started firing rockets at lawyers." He shook his head. "No. Nothing for me there. I'm happy here thank you very much."

Hooper strode out and caught up with Smith. They continued walking together. "If this is what you call being happy I'd hate to see you when you're sad."

They eventually reached Smith's glass fronted, refrigerated paradise. They'd restocked! Hooper watched in amazement as Smith dug deep in his pocket, produced a raft of change and one by one bought every single coffee glazed doughnut in the machine. He just stood there, fed in change, typed F-8 and waited for the doughnut to arrive in the slot on its little greaseproof paper square. Then he took it out, added it to the small pile on the coffee table behind him and repeated the action. At one point he produced a ten spot and asked Hooper if he had any change.

Once Smith had satisfied himself that no one else on the entire base was going to get one of his precious coffee ring drug, he stood back and let Hooper take a look over the offerings. He muttered his discontent. "Damn it. The one flavour I want and I can never find it in these machines."

"What topping do you like?" said Smith, biting down on his first doughnut before they'd even left the vending area.

"Well, I had it once in D.C. and I haven't been able to find it since. Banana."

Smith nearly choked on his mouth full and Hooper had to slap his back in order to bring him back to normality. After Smith had stopped coughing and spluttering, Hooper asked, "You OK?"

"Yeah." choked Smith. "It's just that if you had joined me for doughnuts a week ago, they had it in."

Hooper scowled. "Just my damn luck." Once he was convinced that Smith wasn't going to choke to death, Hooper turned to the machine and settled for a plain vanilla iced ring. When it was delivered, they walked back to ops; Hooper munching on his rare treat and Smith carrying an arm full of his usual fair. Hooper was sure they would melt before Smith managed to get through even a quarter of them. After all, there was a reason why the vending machine was refrigerated.

He reflected that maybe his offer to Smith had come too late anyway; his mental health was now clearly in question. Hooper had seen drug addition, alcohol addition, self harm; hell, he thought he'd seen people with a mental reliance on every possible substance under the sun, but glazed doughnuts was a new one on him.

He'd seen grown men brought down by cocaine; women turned to living skeletons by heroine; but ... yeast?!

When they emerged into the centre once more, Smith dumped the doughnuts on the desk and arranged them quickly into neat little piles. Hooper took a look at the screen and noticed that it wouldn't be long now before the communication drone would be over Roswell. "Any sign of the Hydra?" he asked.

"No, Sir."

"Have we got sight of Jefferson's team?"

"Yes Sir." The drone feed of the three of them on the roof was brought up on the screen. The team were actively looking at the drone so they knew that something was happening; they just didn't know what.

"Communication drone in range, Sir. We should be able to talk with them."

Hooper keyed the mike. "Can you hear me Jefferson?"

"Yes Sir." came the reply. "Duds, you on?"

"I'm here. On the roof of Wells Fargo. No sign of the robot."

Hooper put forward the situation. "We're in a holding pattern now. No idea where the robot is or what to do next. The communications drone is throwing a lot of energy into the comms so it will have to pull back to refuel occasionally. That means black spots as we don't have a second to replace it. If anyone has any ideas, pipe up."

Silence. No one had a clue what to do next.

Hawkeye said his piece, "Our only two options remain; to get a round down the back of its neck or else lure it into explosives I reckon."

No one challenged him or offered an alternative, so his words hung in everyone's ears. Jefferson eventually narrowed down the options. "Well I'm still its target, so in lieu of not knowing where it is, the only option left is to trap it." Again, no challenge. "Duds, any ideas?"

"Give me a while to think."

"Smith, can you locate any possible sites?"

"Muph uump."

"What?"

Smith hastily chewed and swallowed his mouthful of doughnut. "I'll get to work on it."

While they were sitting there pondering, Hooper laid in a call to City Hall to keep an eye open for anything that might help them. There was more than one wireless camera around the town so the robot might have repeated the same trick somewhere else.

"General," continued Jefferson, "can you arrange to get some food dropped to Duds and us? I don't know about anyone else but the sound of Smith eating is reminding me that the last thing I had was a power bar at the trailer."

"Consider it done. Anything else?" There was more than enough time for a helicopter to drop them some supplies.

"Yes please. Some rifles and ammo would go down a treat. Whatever weapons are in the Military Institute are probably well past their use by date."

"On their way."

Duds chimed in, "The Pecos river is to the east of here. What say we do the old, blow up the bridge while it's crossing it routine?"

Smith pulled up a map and took a look. He poured water on Dud's splashing idea. "The bridge is too short and not very high. The speed of the Hydra would see it safely across before you could push the button and even if you did, the drop wouldn't do it any damage. Nice try, though."

"What say we fry it? A few thousand volts or something." offered Hilly.

"Heard of double insulation?" said Hawkeye.

"Well multiply that a few times. The armour has different layers. That's part of its secret sauce."

"What if we drop something heavy on its head like they did with a piano in the cartoons?" said Hooper.

Jefferson picked that one up. "With all due respect Sir, the foolish ideas are supposed to come from the rank and file. Duds, would you care to officially make the same observation that our superior officer just made so we can ridicule it please?"

"Don't be a wise ass Jefferson." snapped Hooper.

"Sorry, Sir. Humour is how I keep myself level in a tough spot."

"Well, they don't get much tougher than this." said Hilly, picking at the surface of the roof.

Silence descended for a while longer.

Duds came forward, "You know there might be some mileage in that weight dropping idea. The only thing the robot's got left is the sniper rifle and it can't shoot at the air any more. How about it?"

Smith piped up. "Unlikely. Even with all its tyres shot it would still be agile enough to dodge anything you dropped on it. The design crew paid special attention to the wheels as they were the obvious weak point."

Off the radio, Hooper asked Smith, "What about more air to surface missiles?"

Smith tapped away at a terminal and pulled up the last fault report on the robot. Most of the sensor array was still intact. "No, it would still detect them and with the buildings around there, coupled with its speed, it could redirect a missile into a building quite easily. You'd practically have to level Roswell, before you could get a clear shot at it."

Hooper put his hand on Smith's shoulder and said despondently, "We're not far away from that option already."

As they continued to sit there, time marched on and helicopters arrived on site with boxes slung underneath them. They dropped their cargo onto the roofs of both the repair shop and the bank, kicking up a load of dust and making a hell of a racket as they did so. Not that anyone particularly cared; what was a bit of noise if it was bringing food and ammo. The teams ripped them open and took a look at what was inside. Unsurprisingly the ration packs were the first things they went for and then, with sated stomachs, they picked through the rest of the supplies. A couple more SCAR-H rifles, ammo and a rocket launcher. There were some spare batteries for the radios, some water and blankets for the nights.

"Duds." Jefferson called over the radio. "You got a rocket launcher in yours?"

"Yes boss. You thinking what I'm thinking?"

"Why not! Smith, can you run the numbers on these things? General, if the rocket launchers will do the job is there any chance of getting some extra soldiers in here to lend a hand?"

Almost as a man, Hooper and Smith said, "OK." and Smith paged Professor Hicks. He knew Hicks was a very clever man, so either he wouldn't be very far away or he was already on a shuttle to Mars.

Hooper went back to his area and took a look at the detailed map of Roswell centre. "There's a cluster of buildings where Tilden crosses Main. If this idea was a goer we could put enough men on those roofs with launchers and deliver enough fire power at one shot to possibly kill it."

Hawkeye joined in, "With the sniper rifle limited they should be relatively safe as well; except that they'll be on top of the explosions."

The teams chewed on their ration packs while Arizona ran the numbers. Eventually, Hooper came back on the radio. "Right. Hicks has done the sums. We're going to drop eight men with rocket launchers in that area. Jefferson, when we're ready you need to ride your bike in to the middle of it all and stay there. We'll tell the robot were you are and when it comes for you, you ride like hell."

Jefferson responded. "Sounds like a plan."

Hooper finished the line of thought. "Right. It'll take me some time to get this organised so you folks take the afternoon to recover and we'll meet up on channel tomorrow morning. Everyone happy with that?"

Jefferson responded simply, "Yes, Sir."

Duds also responded. "Loud and clear, Sir."

"OK." Hooper continued. "We're signing off but you've got another hour before the radio drone needs to refuel. The surveillance drones are going to keep searching for the robot throughout the day. See you tomorrow morning, 08:00 sharp."

With Arizona signed off that just left the team on the radio.

Jefferson announced, "Duds, do you want to

come over here and join us? We're not far north."

"If it's all the same to you boss, I'd rather just be alone on this roof for a while."

Everyone understood where he was coming from. He still needed to mourn Bunny; as they all did. "Sure. Well, you know where we are if you want us."

"OK. See you tomorrow."

Everyone signed off and settled down to spend the rest of the afternoon in their positions.

Duds sat on Wells Fargo, ripped open an energy bar and chewed at its contents while he looked out over Roswell. It consisted mostly of low, one storey buildings in a very regimented pattern. Almost like a chess board. Here and there were other buildings like churches and official offices, which were more grand and stuck out boldly on the horizon.

Like many towns of its type there were areas of heavy concrete and mixed in, were lines of trees running along the roads. He could see swimming pools in some peoples gardens and everything was so peaceful and quiet that he found himself just enjoying the view.

As the sun started to go down and the sky turned a glorious orange, a few more tears rolled down his cheek as his memory flipped back through the years and the good natured banter that he shared with Bunny. She never so much as fired a bullet at anyone. Tough words and steel-eyed glances sure, but she never hurt a fly. There were probably a few radar dishes that would disagree with his account of Bunny's peaceful nature, but what they hell did they matter.

189

The other three elected to stay on the roof. Nowhere, really, to go. Nothing to talk about either. They all *wanted* to talk about Bunny and reminisce but the pain was still too raw.

Jefferson looked at an increasingly worried Hilly, "Don't panic, I'm still the bait." He smiled a little but she saw that behind his eyes there was a very real expectation that he might not make it out of this alive.

Silence reigned for another few minutes before Jefferson pointed at Hawkeye's trousers. "I recognise those." he said. "Mannheim?"

"Well same pair but different, obviously."

"Yeah, obviously." he chuckled. "Not much made it out of that dryer in one piece!" All three of them laughed at the memory of the launderette escapade.

Hilly chimed in, "Do you remember the look on the chef's face! Dust and broken tiles all over his kitchen. I thought he was going to explode!" They chuckled as they remembered the minor chaos of the event.

Slowly the laughter between them died down and they became a little melancholy. Not having the same height as Duds they couldn't marvel at the city-scape, but they did have a good view of the golf course and the trees as darkness gently fell and the air around them turned cooler. Jefferson decided to wear the balaclava to keep his head warm overnight. For some reason the colour didn't bother him any more; he was proud to wear it. The vehicle repair shop they were camped on gave them basic toilet and washing facilities; so once they had cooked up some ration packs and felt more comfortable, they moved inside, wrapped themselves in the emergency blankets and got an uneasy sleep.

The following day at 08:00 everyone was on the radio. Hooper had put the call out and eight soldiers had come forward. They were fitted out with as much body armour as practical, to survive the combined rocket blasts and dropped, by helicopter, on to the roofs of shops by Tilden. They painted a line in the road where, once the robot crossed it, they were all to fire as one. Then they measured out two other lines which they painted further away in the road. If the robot reached those markers then the angle of elevation would be enough so it could shoot them. When it got outside those lines they were to duck for cover.

Some bright spark asked what they were to do if the robot came at them from the side instead of straight down the road, but he received a dressing down and was told that if that happened, he should just kiss his ass goodbye. That warning stopped any further questions.

By early afternoon all was ready and Hooper gave the signal. Duds was still on top of Wells Fargo on look out, and there wasn't really any need for Hilly or Hawkeye to go anywhere so they could stay on the roof. For the sake of his own conscience, Hawkeye asked if he could take station in the Alien Zone, so that he could have a shot at the back of the robot's neck if it happened to pass his way. Jefferson denied him on the grounds it might distract the robot from the rocket launchers.

He hugged them both farewell on the off-chance that he didn't make it back. In case the robot was watching on CCTV he kept Bunny's balaclava on his head. No sense in starting the party early. Then he climbed down from the building and got on the motocross bike once more. Quarter of a tank of fuel left. More than enough. Kicking the engine into action he sped away down Main, with Hilly and Hawkeye watching him go. He hadn't taken any weapons so that he could ride fast and light. All they could do now was wait.

Jefferson was on high alert as he travelled down Main. If the robot popped its head out too soon then it would be game over. He felt his heart pound harder in his chest as he approached the debris at the Alien Zone. He slowed up and rode through it, thanking his lucky stars that he was riding the motocross. If he wasn't, then he'd have to go around it and that would lose him … well, what would it lose him? He didn't know. He wasn't thinking straight now and that worried him.

It didn't take long to get over the rubble and make his way a little further south to the centre of the fire zone. He nodded at some of the soldiers that he could see semi-hidden on the roof tops. They were covered in padding and wearing ear defenders, so it was pointless shouting at them. It was an open road from North to South and Jefferson felt a strange sense of vulnerability but also at peace. It was as if this was where he was meant to be. He looked down the road at the painted lines. They didn't look to be that far away. At the pace that the Hydra could move, he wondered whether it would be possible for the timings to work out. Well, it was too late to worry about that now. "OK," he said. "In position."

"Right Smith," said Hooper, "Give his co-ordinates to the robot."

A few key taps was all it took and everyone was on the look out. Suspense filled the air as people waited with bated breath for the robot to reveal itself.

There was a rumble and a crash from the building beneath Hawkeye and Hilly. They stood up and looked in puzzlement. The robot sped out of an open rolling door in the side of the building and headed down the road that Jefferson had gone down moments before. "Hell!" exclaimed Hilly. "It was beneath us the whole time!"

"How?"

"The maintenance bay doors were open."

"Bloody electrical, silent fucking motors." swore Hawkeye. He felt like he'd been cheated of a viable second chance and he waved his fist at the distant dot that the robot had become as it raced towards Jefferson. He was furious at how they had missed it.

Jefferson told them to calm down. It was out of their hands now. At least he knew it was coming in from the north and it was coming in hot. He saw the speck of the robot as it approached down Main. He gunned the engine and sped south, hoping that the Alien Zone rubble would slow it up enough so that he wouldn't be in range of the rifle and it would give the soldiers a better chance of hitting it with the rocket launchers.

With his head bent over the handlebars, he

opened up the throttle as far as it would go and screamed the motocross bike down the street. He didn't look back but he heard the massive explosion of eight rocket launchers behind him as they found their target.

The robot emerged from the gigantic cloud of fire and tarmac, skidded itself around and changed the direction of its motors trying to drive backwards, while still being able to shoot at the soldiers. When it hit the magic line they all ducked. With no targets to shoot at, the robot spun around again and resumed its pursuit of Jefferson.

Jefferson, however, had turned off Main the moment he heard the explosion and did a long U turn back north again as soon as he could.

"Another damage report, Sir." offered an operative.

Hooper and Smith were at her side like a shot. "What is it?"

"Decoding it now." She leafed through the code book. "It's deaf. The explosions took out the microphones, and the infra red camera is also out of action. Some of its radio scanners are out as well."

"Yes!" said Smith, pumping his arm in the air. "Jefferson, the robot can't hear your bike engine. Just stay out of its sight and you'll stand a chance."

These were the most nail biting moments of Jefferson's life. The robot was heading south and the motocross was heading north on adjoining streets. With every cross road, Jefferson's heart skipped a beat as he looked nervously to his right. His hands were sweating with the pressure and his breathing was strained. If the robot saw him now, then he was all out of tricks. Out of the blue, he recognised that he was actually on Second again and had definitely passed the robot without being seen. "Made it out alive, Sir."

"Good. Now keep your head down and find somewhere to camp out. It was underneath you guys undetected at the repair shop before, so don't go back there now. The communications drone needs refuelling which will take a couple of hours, so we're going to be out of touch for a while."

Everyone acknowledged and signed off. Hooper gave the order for the helicopters to extract the soldiers while they still had enough light and knew where the Hydra was. He could only hope that Jefferson found somewhere safe in the meantime.

"So, why didn't those rockets destroy the thing?" Hooper posed the obvious question to Smith.

"Speed probably. It was most likely just too fast for your men to aim at it. Don't you have any automatic launchers?"

Hooper harked Smith's memory back a few days, "If you recall the tank battle at the border it was moving too fast even for them to track it."

"Then we're going to keep having the same problem until we can find a way to slow it down somehow."

Hooper wasn't going to let Smith completely off the hook. "Hang on a minute. This is AMARS we're stood in. Don't you have anything that can deliver a payload accurately enough to stop that thing?"

"Nope. If you don't buy it, we don't make it."

He added, somewhat unhelpfully, "I dare say we can knock something together in a year or two if you want."

Hooper slapped his forehead with his hand. Wasn't anything straightforward in this place? As he stood there trying to come to terms with this ridiculous situation, he found himself having a strange urge; one that he realised was the start of a slippery slope. From deep within the subconscious corners of his mind, he had a sudden desire to walk the blue carpet to the doughnut machine.

Chapter 16
Pressure Cooker

Jefferson rode the motocross bike slowly up an alley behind some shops. He reflected that perhaps he shouldn't have been so hard on Hilly when she kitted up, because now he felt like he needed to do the same. He wanted some arms; something to keep him safe in the midst of the insanity that this whole damn situation had become. Rationally, he knew that nothing he was likely to get his hands on would even make a scratch on the robot, but emotion was starting to leak into his thoughts and affect his decision making. Right now he just wanted something that would bolster his confidence and make him feel like he actually stood a chance in hell.

As he rode, he checked out the company names on the back doors. One was called, 'Personal Protection,' so he decided to give it a try. Stopping the bike, he tried the door. Miraculously, it was open. He killed the engine and pushed the bike inside. "Hello?"

"Hey dude!" came a voice from the front of the shop. "Why don't you use the front door like everyone else?" It was the voice of a slim man with long hair, in his early twenties, dressed in jeans and T-shirt. He came through the beaded curtain and into the back of the shop.

"Well, there's a killing machine out there, which sort of makes it hard to use the main street if you know what I mean."

"Ah!" said the man knowingly. "Yeah, that's why you need Personal Protection!" he smiled and puffed out his chest, on which was the company logo. I'm your personal assistant today. The name's Geoff." said Geoff, pointing at his name badge. "Follow me."

Geoff went back through the beaded curtain to the front of the shop and Jefferson, full of hope, followed him. They emerged in to a room with shelves of things that Jefferson didn't think he would ever lay eyes on. He was stunned. Geoff mistook his new customers silence for awe and, proud as ever of his little empire, he gave Jefferson the full spiel waving his arms in large gestures while he talked. "We've got it all. Need luck on your side? We have rabbits feet of all sizes, on everything from key rings to money pouches. Worried about what the government is doing with your thoughts? Well just wear a cap like this." He lifted a baseball cap from a nearby shelf to reveal that the inside was lined with tin foil. "We stock a complete range even up to straw sun hats, all lined to keep your personal brain waves personal. If you know what I mean."

Jefferson couldn't believe it. If it was supernatural or superstitious it was in here. Blessed Crucifix's, dream catchers, Kachina Dolls, crystals, talismans and amulets filled the shelves. The few free spaces on the walls were filled with pentagrams, tables and charts that talked about the various colours of protection, alongside slate tablets with the Eye of Horus, presumably for hanging on the front door. There was even a full body suit made from a thicker foil. He couldn't resist. "What's that for?"

"Ah, that stops the government from moving your body by microwave. Did you know that some people have strangled themselves in their sleep? They say that's how the government gets their enemies to kill themselves when they least expect it. Go to bed in this, and they can't control your limbs." Geoff slowly nodded his head in awe and concern at the technological skill and prowess of their all-controlling, authoritative agencies.

Jefferson just looked at him, his mouth agape. This certainly wasn't the kind of personal protection he had been thinking of when he walked in to the place. He had expected things like guns, grenades, rape spray, that sort of thing. Eventually, he shook his head and brought himself back to reality. Geoff was looking at him, expecting his new customer to tell him all about whatever paranoid and spiritual concerns needed to be assuaged. Jefferson decided to play on this and see what Geoff could actually do for him. "Tell you what I do need; somewhere safe."

"Ah! Safe from what, exactly?"

"Well, from everything really. Government forces, strange micro-waves of bodily control, bad spirits, I mean, if the alarm sounded for the end of the world, where would you go?"

"It already did, man. The government have a killer robot out there right now, as we speak. Remember?" That answered Jefferson's question. Disaster had already struck and Geoff was in his store with all the lucky charms and protection things, secure in the belief that they would save him from a bullet to the brain. OK, so perhaps this was a bad line of questioning.

Jefferson leant on the counter. "So, what about any other places? Nuclear shelters? Alien abduction free zones?" he shrugged his shoulders. "Anything like that around?"

Geoff thought for a bit. "Nah. Aliens are aliens. There's not much you can do against death rays." His eyes went blank for a moment as he turned his thoughts inwards and then he chuckled to himself. "There was one dude who was lunatic enough to think he could defend himself from aliens. Old Harrison."

"Yeah?" Jefferson figured that things couldn't get much crazier than they were already, so he prompted Geoff for more info. After all, it wasn't as if there was anywhere he needed to be at the moment. "Tell me about Old Harrison." he enquired, leaning on the counter and feigning interest.

Geoff ducked behind the counter and there was a rustling sound. After a few moments, he surfaced again with what looked like a map of a field. "Here you go." Geoff switched back in to his element, which seemed to be conspiracy theories and wild beliefs. "Now, Harrison was really concerned about aliens getting to him, so he bought himself a field out east on Nineteenth. Built a small house in the middle, surrounded the place with deep holes and then covered them up. He reckoned that if the aliens came after him, he could get himself in the hut and they'd fall in the holes and get trapped."

"Really?!" Jefferson was intrigued.

"Yeah! Really! I mean, the guy was a total

loon!" Geoff leaned back and smiled. "Everybody knows that if aliens get here from outer space, then falling down a hole isn't going to stop them! They can just fly out of a hole like that." Geoff was starting to make Jefferson uneasy and the disparaging way he was talking of Harrison, was a case of the pot calling the kettle black.

Jefferson sighed as he turned the map towards him and started to study it. "So, anyway," he said, "these holes; how deep are they?"

"Oh, something like twenty feet or so."

"And the sides..."

Geoff looked at the map and did some rough calculations with his fingers from some magical scale that only he knew. "I reckon that's a good eight foot at the narrowest; fifteen wide."

This was starting to sound like it might hold some promise. "What happened to Harrison? Is he out there now?"

"Oh no!" said Geoff, stepping back and shaking his head. "No, no, no. He vanished a few months ago. Word was that he went to California when his lottery ticket came up." Geoff slowly leaned forward and tapped his nose. "But folks in the know say he's the latest abductee." He slowly nodded his head in a conspiratorial manner.

Jefferson leaned back, wanting to put some distance between himself and Geoff. "Abducted by who?" he challenged.

"Ah; now that, we don't know. But people vanish and then turn up again out of the blue all the time, so someone's behind all this." He paused for effect, "Or some-*thing*."

Jefferson sighed. He knew he shouldn't have asked. Still, he needed to press on. "Yeah, OK. So who's out there now?"

"No one. Still exactly how he left it. He hasn't been gone long. If the aliens keep to their usual schedule, he'll be back in a couple more months. He'll tell everyone he blew the money on wine, women and song; but we'll all know the truth." Geoff started slowly nodding his head again.

This was starting to send Jefferson's bullshit-o-meter in to overload but he caught himself before he said something that he would later regret. Instead he managed, "Mind if I sit down a while?"

"Sure. Take the weight off. No one else has come in here since that robot showed up."

Jefferson was starting to ponder about getting the robot trapped down one of those holes at the Harrison place. They were big enough, sure. But were they deep enough? Would the Hydra be able to climb its way back out again with its various arms and tools? Even if it could, how much time would it take to figure out what it needed to do? Would it be long enough to lob a bomb in and blow it to kingdom come? It certainly seemed to be the only way to slow it up, long enough to hit it with something meaningful.

The more he sat there and thought about it, not only did it sound feasible, but it also seemed to be the only option that was left. Everything else had failed. But the question remained as to how he'd get it into the trap. As he was the bait, he'd need some way to stay alive long enough to get it in there. That's where his plan fell down.

The robot was down to its sniper rifle, sure, but it was still very effective with it on the level. If he could stop it from being able to target him then he might stand a chance. If he couldn't then there was no point in even trying. He'd be dead before the robot needed to set a single wheel onto the Harrison patch. He sat back and waited for the radio to come back on-line.

As he sat there and thought, he eyed the various things on offer, while Geoff eyed him. He pondered that he could do with a little bit of luck around about now. OK, he caught himself, a barrow load of it. A shop load of it even! Ha! He wondered if there was any harm in having a rabbits foot to try and change fate. Then he caught himself again. That way lay madness. After all, the rabbit hadn't been so lucky and it had four feet to begin with.

Rabbits. He thought again of Bunny. She didn't deserve that sort of death. He started to chide himself for not realising she could have been a target. If only he'd been more on the ball then maybe she'd still be alive.

"You want some noodles, man?"

Jefferson snapped out of it. "No thanks. I've eaten."

"Ok, I'm just going out the back." Geoff got up and went through the curtain. He still kept a casual eye on Jefferson through the beads. Not that he needed to. There was no reason for Jefferson to move from where he was. Time ticked on, Geoff made and ate his noodles and they sat there in relative silence.

Everyone got a bit of a jolt when their radios

sparked back in to life. "You guys there?" asked Hooper. One by one they called in present and correct. "Anyone got any news?"

Jefferson responded. "Well I've got a plan B, or C, or whatever it is we're on now."

"I hope it's a good one, 'cause I'm flat out of ideas." said Hilly. Jefferson made a mental note to get her some extended leave and an appointment with a psychiatrist once all this was over. Dealing with the robot had spooked her really badly.

He brought himself up and leant forward as he discussed the Harrison place with the team. "Is there any other place like this with loads of holes?"

Smith looked at Hooper as he went over the maps on his wall. Hooper turned and shook his head. "No, it looks like the Harrison place is the only option. How many holes are there?"

Jefferson looked at the map. "Well I reckon it could fall down any one of twelve. But there is still one rather serious problem to overcome."

A silence permeated the radio for a few moments before Hilly asked the obvious. "What's the problem?"

"Getting the robot to follow me onto the land instead of just shooting me from a distance with that damn sniper rifle. Smith, can you ask Hicks if he's got any ideas?"

"Sure."

"Duds, do you have any shaped charge left?"

"Yeah, loads. I disassembled the original trap, remember?"

"If we managed to get that robot down a hole, can you blow it to hell when it's down there?"

"That's doable, yes. But I don't have enough explosive to line all the holes. Plans a no go unless we can get more shipped in. About four times what we used in the first trap."

Hawkeye chimed in. "What if you make a charge and throw it down the hole after the robot?"

Things went quiet for a while and then Duds piped up. "Leave it to me. I know just what to do."

Jefferson queried, "How much time do you need?"

"Give me a garden centre and an hour."

"Well you've got all the time in the world. We've still got to solve that last problem of stopping its rifle."

Smith came back on the line. "Hicks says that the sniper rifle works on laser targetting, so unless you can find some way to run faster than the speed of light then you don't stand much chance."

"Damn it." cursed Jefferson. "What if I get to the Harrison place and you give it the coordinates again?"

Professor Hicks came on the line. "If you were already on the property it would analyse the ground and find the holes. Whatever you do has to be fluid, so that it doesn't have the time to stop and, er... think. That's the only hope you'd stand."

Jefferson sat there bashing his head against a metaphorical brick wall. There had to be some way to do this. He absent mindedly stared at things around the shop while his mind turned in circles. Eventually, his sight locked on something and a light bulb went off in his head. "I've got it. Damn it, I've got it. Duds, let me know when you're ready.

Everyone else, stand by."

"OK boss." came the responses.

Jefferson gestured to Geoff to get his attention. "That all in one anti government control suit thingy. How much?"

An hour and a half later, Jefferson pushed the bike out of the back door of the shop, dressed head to toe in the silver suit with its hood pulled over the pink balaclava. Sitting behind the front zipper was a copy of the plans to the Harrison place. On the one hand he felt like a complete fool dressed like that. On the other, he was a man on a mission and this was Roswell after all. He had a plan. Not much of a plan but it was all that he had and, insane as it was, it just might work.

With renewed energy, he kicked the engine in to action and rode north east. The field wasn't too far away from the treatment plant he had sheltered at earlier so he was confident that he'd be able to get there with no issue.

That was how he came to find himself out east on Nineteenth, at the entrance to a large field with a small shack in the centre of it. Harrison had apparently been gone for some months so the grass in the field was nice and thick. All the better for hiding the holes. He studied the map and memorised their positions. Failure at this stage would mean certain death.

He keyed his mic. "You ready, Duds?"

"Ready boss." Duds was waiting in his hiding place at a car dealership. He was parked among some camper vans that would shield him from the robot if it passed his way. As it was still in the lower part of town looking for Jefferson, there was a fair chance that it would sail right by his position. However at the speeds that it went, there would be little chance it would stop to shot him, even when he did start the bike and follow it.

"OK Hooper, transmit those co-ordinates to the robot and when it's taken the bait, shut off the mainframe so it can't ask for more help. Everyone, keep your eyes peeled. It's now or never." Jefferson checked that the silver hood was pulled tight over the top of the balaclava. With the exception of his face and the soles of his boots he was now completely silver.

He didn't have long to wait. Hooper piped up, "The drones show the robot moving north. Looks like it's headed out to you now at speed."

The robot zoomed past Duds position at a scary pace and as it did so, Duds kicked his engine into life. "It's on its way." Jefferson looked over his shoulder and saw the distant dot of the robot getting rapidly larger.

He gunned the motocross engine and heard the whistle of a bullet as it passed his head. It was just as he'd hoped. The laser couldn't target his reflective suit properly and the robot was having problems trying to shoot him.

The sound of a second bullet was his signal to ride onto the field as fast as he dare, while swerving around the slightly odd pattern of markings. If he fell down one of these holes himself then it was game over, for good.

As he scrambled his way forward, the robot pulled up at the road side and tried once more to aim the sniper rifle at Jefferson. It just couldn't get a lock on him. As Jefferson was riding over the lumpy field, the silver suit was bouncing the laser all over the place and the robot wasn't able to target, so it did the next best thing and shot his tyre out.

Jefferson knew that if he got any mud on the suit then he was as good as dead, so he let the bike fly out from under him and did his utmost to stay on his feet. Breathing hard, he yelped in pain as one of his ankles sprained while he tried to regain his footing, but he had to keep running.

As Jefferson half ran, half hobbled through the field trying to remember where the holes were, his life started flashing before his eyes. This must surely be the end. There was no way he'd make it to the hut in time and, even if he did, the wooden hut would be no protection from the killing machine behind him.

The Hydra tried to talk to the mainframe but Smith had stopped it from sending any replies. The robot had to make a decision on its own and it decided that if it couldn't kill Jefferson with bullets, then it would have to catch him and do the job itself.

It started to drive onto the field and, as he heard it start to move, Jefferson yelped again and tried to run faster towards the hut. His tactic worked and the Hydra made a bee line for him, falling straight down one of the holes.

When Jefferson heard the almighty crash he let out a hideous cry of pain, joy and hysteria, but it wasn't until he heard Dud's engine that he dared to turn his head around to see what had happened. "It's down!" he yelled, "It's bloody well down!" as he hopped with joy.

"Yeah, well we've still got to finish the job." responded Duds as he brought the bike to the edge of the hole and looked down into it. The Hydra was flailing various arms around trying to work out what was happening. It was throwing all sorts of questions to the mainframe to try and get a handle on what fate had befallen it, and what action to take, but Smith had cut off all the responses. Still, it would only be a matter of time before it would work it out for itself. Duds could see it was already starting to manoeuvre itself the right way up.

"Get on. Fast." said Duds as he reached into one of his saddlebags and tossed something into the hole. Jefferson hobbled as fast as he could to the bike, uttering a mixture of half scream and half manic laughter as he did so. "Hurry up!" Duds encouraged him. "We don't have much time."

Jefferson used his good leg to stabilise himself as he threw the other one across the back seat of the bike. He grabbed Duds around the waist and in pain, yelled, "Yeaargh!" which Duds took as a sign he was on and ready. Revving the bike, Duds rode off the grass and down the road a few hundred yards before skidding around and looking back at the field, where they could still hear the robot struggling against the sides of the hole.

Then, for a moment there was silence. The robot stopped and stared at what Duds had dropped in to the pit.

Back in the operations room the operative responsible for the network called out. "Sir, the robot has sent an identity request to the mainframe. It's trying to work out whether an object is a threat."

Hooper mopped his brow and Smith took up the challenge. "What's the item?"

The operative stared in disbelief at the image that the robot had sent back. "I think it's looking at a fat, pink, fluffy bunny rabbit, Sir."

Jefferson couldn't see the look on Duds' face but he had a very good guess that it was the cold mask of revenge. What he *could* see, however, was Duds thumb as he flipped open the safety cover on his trigger buttons and pressed one of them.

A massive explosion came from the hole. Steam, earth and metallic robot parts filled the sky as the Hydra became one of the most expensive pressure cookers in history. They both sat motionless on the bike as pieces of metal and electronic circuit boards started raining down from the sky.

Somehow, despite the very real possibility that one of those stray pieces could easily have landed on their heads and knocked them senseless, they were both just content to watch the debris as it fell. A sense of relief flowed through them as their most dangerous nemesis had finally been defeated. Against all odds, they'd done it.

The death of the robot was seen on the screens in Arizona and the blast was heard by Hilly and Hawkeye on the roof. Anyone would have been forgiven for screaming in joy at a hard won victory but instead there was silence. Hearts hung heavy at the loss of good lives in a battle that they shouldn't have had to fight. A foe of their own creation. It should never have come to this.

The moment was captured perfectly, however, when Duds keyed his mike and simply announced, "Check mate."

Chapter 17
Goodbye

The four of them, along with Hooper and a few other soldiers, were stood in the peaceful, picturesque location that was Arlington National Cemetery, Virginia. Bunny's remains had been recovered. Jefferson had wanted to know more on this but Hooper had declined to go in to detail. She was buried will full military honours and the remaining four, dressed in their finery, said their pieces. Despite their years of service and being among the toughest the army had to offer, tears were shed and chests were taut as she was lowered gently into the ground.

Among the accounts of past engagements and battles won was the teams feeling that, as the youngest of them she should have been the last to go, not the first. They hoped that wherever she was now, that they had large RV's with quirky bumper stickers, soldering irons and electronics stores. Duds choked back his tears as he apologised to her, for finally carrying through his threat to blow her fluffy rabbit to bits, but that it seemed like the right thing to do at the time.

The team did another mission, but without Bunny it wasn't the same and the army let them retire gracefully as thanks for their years of hard work in tight situations.

Roswell recovered relatively quickly. Within a few weeks the majority of the damage had been repaired. The Army had poured in resources to fix the worst of it, so there wasn't that much for the press to pick through once the exclusion had been lifted. A few buildings still had scaffolding around them, but that only served to support canvas so no one could easily see what was going on behind.

The P.R. people worked their magic by sowing contradictory theories about trialling new missile defence systems and laughing off the rogue robot theories with, "Really? We've got kill switches for those things, you know!" When all that was mixed up with the partial reports from everyone else along with the fact that a number of the witnesses were already well known conspiracy theorists, the rest of the country just scratched its head. In the end the conclusion was that, like many things that the military got up to, they would likely never know the real truth. And that was how the escapades of a killer robot on the loose just became another part of the Roswell legend.

When Duds quit the unit he started up his own small garage dealing in motorbikes. He didn't specialise in any particular brand but even though he was no longer hauling explosives around, he still preferred the jumbo saddlebags.

Hawkeye became a slightly unusual pest control officer, just to keep his shooting eye in. There weren't that many people in his trade who dispatched rodents with fifty calibre rounds.

Hilly bought herself a bar and within a week of running it, became tea total. There was a rumour that she had changed drastically and that this was her way of sticking two fingers up at the military part of her life. Then again, there was the contradictory and more likely theory that she realised the inevitable; that if she carried on the way she was going she'd drink all the profits and go bankrupt. Her bar was also equipped with a top of the range wide screen TV that she didn't watch.

Jefferson found himself a quiet corner in a back water town and settled down for a peaceful retirement. After he arrived the local press started reporting about a strange, silver ghost-like creature with a pink head, that would appear every Halloween and scare the hell out of the kids as they went round doing their trick or treating.

Smith retired from AMARS. He had a complete mental breakdown and spent some time on a psychiatric ward before being discharged with a full pension. There was a rumour circulating that the final straw was when he received an invoice for the repair of bullet holes in golf carts. However no one seemed to be able to track the existence of such an invoice, let alone any record of it being paid. When he was released from the psychiatric unit, he moved into town and started a business selling traditional doughnuts, made the old fashioned way; whatever that meant.

Gina won a junior place on the Hydra team and eventually worked her way up the ranks to replace Hicks, who sadly passed away from a heart attack after trying to referee one too many heated team discussions. Only time would tell whether that promotion was a blessing, or a curse.

Andy used hypnotherapy to overcome his fear of live munitions long enough to make an impression with the AMARS big brass, and was moved up the ladder and away from working in the hangers.

Gary carried on being a low level tech in AMARS and lived the rest of his life eating pizza and drinking alcohol. He never did make it in to the world record books, although he was top on the leader board of one or two popular console games.

Hooper was commended for his leadership and ingenuity in the face of adversity, even though it was of the home grown variety, and for the remainder of his service he took great care to ensure that he was never posted anywhere that had any responsibility for monitoring high tech companies, ever again. He did, however, still have Smith on his mind and now that he had time on his hands once more, Hooper determined that he would have to go digging in some records.

THE END

www.ingramcontent.com/pod-product-compliance
Lightning Source LLC
Chambersburg PA
CBHW011500170626
46814CB00008B/2983